'Satan!' Alice scr̶̶̶̶̶̶̶̶̶̶̶̶̶̶̶̶̶̶̶̶̶̶ ̶̶̶̶̶̶̶̶̶̶̶̶̶̶̶̶̶̶̶̶ protect me from you!' She began spitting and snarling at him while scrambling against the wall as if trying to burrow through it and escape.

'What's the background here?' Dr Ferguson asked quickly.

Megan gave him all the details while he stared at Alice and she yelled at him to be gone.

'She won't take the belt off?' he asked.

'No,' Megan said. 'She claims the Devil's in her hand and that he'll attack her heart if she removes it.'

'Right,' he said, 'there's nothing for it. We're going to have to tranquillize her. Diazepam injection, a hundred milligrams . . .'

CASUALTY
HOW IT ALL BEGAN

EVAN CHRISTIE

From the television series created by
Jeremy Brock and Paul Unwin

WARNER BOOKS

A *Warner* Book

First published in Great Britain in 1986 by Grafton Books
This edition published in 1994 by Warner Books

A CIP catalogue record for this book
is available from the British Library.

ISBN 0 7515 0858 6

Printed in England by Clays Ltd, St Ives plc

Warner Books
A Division of
Little, Brown and Company (UK) Limited
Brettenham House
Lancaster Place
London WC2E 7EN

Prologue

Flashing lights . . .

Even now, as she lay on her back in the night-dark street, there were still flashing lights, just like in the disco. Orange flashes, as though the streetlights on either side of the road were leaning over her and winking. A flickering green neon in the window of a record store opposite. And now an electric blue flashing which came closer and closer, and with it the sound of a siren that pierced her to the core.

'Help,' she cried. 'Please help me.'

Her voice sounded distant, as though someone else was speaking the words. The air was thick with petrol and exhaust fumes, and each time she breathed in, there was a twisting pain in her stomach.

'Gary,' she murmured, knowing that she had walked out on her boyfriend at the disco. 'Help me, help me.'

Suddenly a face loomed in front of her – an anxious, bleary-eyed face of a man with blond hair. He didn't look much older than Gary.

'Oh my God,' he said. 'I didn't mean – you came running out of nowhere.'

His face was so close to hers that she could smell his hot, cidery breath. It made her head swim. Then suddenly he was being pushed out of the way by an older man. An ambulance man, she could see from his uniform.

'Don't worry, love,' he said to her. 'Just lie still. We'll have you out of here in no time.'

A wave of relief washed over her. And then the pain

returned, gnawing at her stomach. And now she began to worry. If an ambulance had come for her, it meant that she had been badly injured.

'Help me,' she said again, her voice as distant as before. 'I'm only fifteen.'

And now she was on a stretcher, being lifted up and carried towards the ambulance. She glimpsed the blond-haired man again, standing beside his car – the red Escort that had hit her.

'She shouldn't have run out,' he was saying to a policeman. 'She shouldn't have run out.'

Nearby was a police car, its blue light flashing like a message in Morse Code that she couldn't understand.

'Keep still,' Ewart Plimmer told his patient in a firm but gentle voice as he stitched up the gash over his right eyebrow.

'It's hurting,' the man told him.

'It'll hurt more if you keep wriggling. How did you say you did it?'

'Trod on a fire engine and fell down a few stairs. Cracked my head on the bottom.'

'You *trod* on a fire engine?'

'A toy one. My kid's. She's always leaving things lying about on the floor – ouch, that stings!'

'How old is she?'

'Who?'

'Your daughter.'

'Six. And a right tearaway she is, too.'

Ewart peered down at the man. He was in his late twenties, dressed in a blue anorak and black corduroys. Half my age, Ewart found himself thinking.

'Enjoy her while you can,' he said. 'Things get more difficult as they get older.'

'You got kids?'

'A daughter, like you. But she's eighteen, and still going through the throes of puberty.'

'Gawd,' the man said glumly, 'that's something else for me and the wife to look forward to. Spotty-faced boy-friends and pop music blasting out twenty-four hours a day.'

Ewart smiled. 'You were young once – and not that long ago.'

'Yeah,' came the reply, 'but it seems like ages.'

Young Nurse Simpson passed Ewart a scissors and he trimmed the stitching.

'You finished?' the man said.

'All done,' Ewart replied. By chatting to him, he had taken his mind off the stitching and had been able to complete it with a minimum of fuss.

Nurse Simpson taped a light dressing over the wound. She was on her first night-shift in Casualty, and Ewart had stepped in to help her with the stitching when the man had become agitated.

'That hardly hurt at all,' he said gratefully to Ewart.

'We do our best.'

'Couldn't recommend a good dentist, could you?'

Lying in the back of the ambulance, she felt as if the world was beginning to fade away around her. A voice was talking to her, asking her name, as she hovered between wakefulness and sleep.

What would her parents say? Her father would be furious with her for having gone out in the first place without his permission. When he was angry, he shouted a lot and flecks of spit gathered on his lips. Her mother, anxious and disapproving, would wring her hands and

7

make gulping movements with her mouth, too upset to actually speak.

'It's all right,' a voice was saying to her. 'Just lie still, everything's fine. Can you remember your name? Can you tell me what your name is?'

Jayne, she said, but the word sounded so faint she couldn't be sure whether she'd spoken it aloud or not. *Jayne Witchell, 32 Balfern Grove, Holby, Avon.*

Her parents had a nice house. A detached, red-bricked house with white bay windows and a garage at the side. There were plush carpets and dark antique furniture everywhere. As a child, she was never allowed to walk on the carpets in shoes, or put her hands on the gleaming wood. There was a big new stereo in the front room, but she could only play her records when her father was out. Her mother cleaned up after her everywhere she went, polishing and tidying, throwing out her magazines before she'd even had a chance to read them.

'Can you hear me?' the voice was saying. 'Do you remember your name and address?'

Jayne, she said desperately. *Jayne Witchell* . . .

'It's quiet tonight,' Nurse Simpson remarked.

'Fatal to say that,' Ewart told her, accepting a cup of coffee from her. They were taking a break in the staff room with Nurse Golding, an experienced campaigner in her forties.

Ewart raised his right hand to read his wristwatch, but he had taken it off before washing his hands and forgotten to put it back on. He plucked it out of his trouser pocket. Five past eleven.

'The pubs have just closed,' he told Nurse Simpson, 'and we'll probably get a rush of drunks with cuts and sprains and fractures – especially with it being a Saturday night. A lot can happen between now and seven in the morning.'

She nodded, deferring to his experience. He had been a clinical assistant at the City Hospital in Holby for twenty years, and had spent most of his working life in the city. Because he disliked routine, he'd always found himself relishing tours of duty in the Casualty Department. Life there was unpredictable but seldom dull.

'I hate this shift,' Nurse Golding remarked.

'Well,' said Ewart, 'we're only open on Friday and Saturday nights. I enjoy it myself. And God knows we're needed.'

He sipped his coffee and grimaced.

'I know,' said Nurse Golding. 'It tastes like mud.'

Ewart put the cup down on a white-topped table. 'Something rather nastier than mud, I'd say.'

She showed him a large jar of coffee whose brand name he had never encountered before. 'It's this stuff.'

'What happened to the Nescafé?'

'Economies. We had a memo a few weeks back from Giles Voyce, advising us to make economies "in every possible area". So some bright spark decided that this meant Gold Blend was an indulgence and bought twenty-four jars of that stuff at cost price. We'll be drinking it till Doomsday. Mould Blend, I call it.'

Ewart smiled, but the mention of Voyce had brought a different sort of sour taste to his mouth. Giles Voyce was the hospital's administrator, and there was no love lost between them. Voyce was an earnest proponent of cost-cutting exercises, using every means at his disposal to achieve his aims, irrespective of how this might affect the medical services available to the public. At the same time, he was also a stickler for correct procedure. Two weeks earlier he had carpeted Ewart for operating on a

9

teenage boy who had choked on a fishbone without contacting administration. But to Ewart it had been a purely medical matter, and time was of the essence. The boy had made a good recovery, but without the operation he would have died.

'He's a narrow-minded bureaucrat,' Ewart murmured to himself.

'Who?' asked Nurse Golding.

Ewart looked up, only now aware that he had spoken aloud.

'No one special,' he said. 'Just talking to myself.'

Nurse Golding tut-tutted slowly. 'A bad sign, that.'

'Not at all. It's my favourite method of conversation. At least I know that I'm addressing someone who'll always agree with me.'

Nurse Golding and Ewart grinned, while Nurse Simpson looked puzzled. She had not worked with Ewart before, and was no doubt surprised at the informality which prevailed between staff and surgeon. But Ewart liked it that way. When they were dealing with the public, he was 'Mr Plimmer' to his staff – surgeons were usually 'Mr' rather than 'Dr' – and they deferred to his status and experience, even though he was always open to advice. But he liked them to treat him as a normal human being in the quiet moments between the hurly-burly of hospital work.

Ewart tried another sip of coffee, but the taste was just as revolting as before. Coffee breaks could only be snatched when there were no patients to attend to, but they were very important for the camaraderie of the staff.

'Any sticky labels around?' Ewart asked Nurse Golding.

She thought about it, then went to a filing cabinet near the door. Ewart had spotted an empty coffee jar which had been washed out and was now sitting on the window ledge. There was a handful of paper clips inside. He tipped them out.

Nurse Golding had found a spool of address labels which were sometimes used for sending samples to other departments or hospitals.

'Splendid,' Ewart said, dropping two pound coins from his pocket into the jar. He took a pen from the breast-pocket of his white coat and scribbled on one of the labels. Then he peeled it off its backing paper and stuck it on the jar.

'There,' he said. 'That should start the ball rolling.'

He put the jar in a prominent position on top of the filing cabinet. The label read: CAMPAIGN FOR REAL COFFEE.

She was remembering what had happened in the disco. The stage was pulsing with blue and red and green lights, while Frankie Goes to Hollywood blasted out 'Relax'. She had been dancing with Gary in the smoky, sweaty atmosphere all evening, and only now had she noticed the time.

'I've got to go,' she said suddenly, stopping dancing.

'Why?' said Gary. 'It's only half-ten.'

'My parents'll kill me if I'm late.'

'We can get a taxi back a bit later. I'll pay.'

He was older than her – eighteen, and working for his older brother, a builder. It was he who had persuaded her to go to the disco, even though she was under-age and knew that her parents would never allow it. So she had sneaked out that afternoon without telling them where she was going.

'Come on,' said Gary, 'just another half-hour.'

'I can't.'

'You're not a kid any more. Go home when you feel like it.'

'No,' she insisted. 'Please, Gary, let's go now. We can get a bus at the crossroads.'

She turned and walked off the dance floor to the table where Sandra and her boyfriend, Dean, were sitting. Sandra was seventeen, and she already had a bedsitter of her own. Jayne had gone there that afternoon, changing out of the drab, old-fashioned clothes which her parents made her wear and into a black leather skirt and a white T-shirt scrawled with red Japanese lettering. She'd made herself up with vivid violet eyeliner and black mascara so that she looked five years older than her real age. There'd been no problem getting into the disco. But now she had to change back to the drab young girl for the journey home.

Her clothes were sitting in a Tesco plastic bag on one of the tubular chairs. Flashing colours swirled across the smoked glass of the table-top on which a cluster of empty cocktail glasses stood. Sandra and Dean broke from a clinch as Tears For Fears started singing 'Everybody Wants to Rule the World'.

'What's up?' Sandra asked.

'She wants to go home,' Gary said from behind her.

Jayne didn't like the scornful sound of his voice. Snatching up the carrier bag, she said, 'I'm going to get changed.'

Then she stalked off.

In the washroom she vigorously soaped the make-up from her face, then rubbed it dry in the roll-towel until her cheeks glowed red. She was the fresh-faced fifteen-year-old once more. Well, almost. Hurriedly undressing, she removed the white cotton blouse and the pleated tweed skirt from the bag. Last of all she took out the

12

zippered cardigan which her mother had insisted on knitting for her. It was blue, with multi-coloured snowflakes all over it. Made her look like a refugee from some stupid skiing resort.

As she was stuffing her dancing clothes into the bag, two punk girls entered. They stared at her as they passed, and she was ashamed of what she was wearing, wanting to curl up with embarrassment. She was sure she heard them giggle as she hurried out.

Gary wasn't at the table with Sandra and her boyfriend when she returned to it.

'Keep these safe for me,' she said to Sandra, handing her the carrier bag. She had bought the clothes out of her savings, and her parents had never seen them.

Sandra nodded, but she was staring over Jayne's shoulder towards the dance floor.

The Eurythmics were singing 'Sisters Are Doing It For Themselves', and Gary was dancing with another girl. A pretty-looking girl, with bleached blonde hair and a denim jacket with TAKE IT OR LEAVE IT stitched on the back. Gary was smiling at her, talking and laughing with her.

Jayne felt a wave of betrayal and embarrassment. Suddenly she could not bear to stand there in her stupid clothes a moment longer. She felt as if everyone in the disco was looking at her, laughing at her. Turning, she rushed for the exit.

The doorman gave her a strange look as she hurried past him, but she paid him no heed. Outside the streets were dark and it felt chilly. As she walked along the road towards the bus stop she was almost grateful for her mother's cardigan since it kept out the cold.

But there were tears in her eyes as well. She was certain that Gary was betraying her with the other girl.

TAKE IT OR LEAVE IT. Well, she'd had enough. He was always lording it over her because she was younger than him, and now she was regretting that she'd ever gone to the disco.

Suddenly she realized that she had left her purse in the carrier bag. And her bus was approaching the crossroads. There was a coin in one of the pockets of her cardigan – a fifty pence piece. She gripped it with relief and frantically began running up the road.

The bus was pulling in to the stop. She had to get across the road before it started off again. As she darted out between two parked cars, she saw the Escort rushing towards her. She was stranded in the middle of the road, but there was room for the car to swerve past her, room on either side.

But the driver didn't react. The last thing she saw was his pale face huddled over the wheel, his eyes wide with shock. Even in that instant something told her that he was drunk, too drunk to control the car, *Oh God he's going to hit me!* He didn't even have his headlights on. An instant later there was a terrible thud, and the world lurched around her – lurched and went spinning, lights flashing, engines roaring, as she tumbled helter-skelter across the dark road . . .

'Can you hear me?' came the voice, almost in a whisper.

She could hear him, but she knew she couldn't speak. She was too tired even to open her mouth. A weariness was settling over her, and she welcomed it, let it carry her down into a deep unconsciousness that would blot out the terrible pain in her belly.

'What's the problem here?' Ewart asked as he entered the cubicle.

A man in a well-tailored dark blue suit was standing

14

there, attended by Charlie Fairhead, the Charge Nurse on the night shift that evening. Ewart and Charlie knew one another well and had a mutual respect for one another both professionally and personally. As Charge Nurse – the male equivalent of Sister – Charlie was head of the nursing staff. He was a Londoner in his early thirties who had moved to Holby seven years ago. They had struck up an immediate rapport when they had first worked together, despite their very different temperaments.

'This is Mr Petherham,' Charlie told Ewart. 'He insists on speaking to a doctor.'

Charlie's expression told Ewart: 'awkward customer', though he himself was keeping his cool. Ewart had heard Petherham protesting as he was passing the cubicles where patients were taken for examination. Earlier, he had also overheard Petherham complaining while he was in the waiting area shortly after his arrival. Had he been busy with another patient, he would have insisted – politely but firmly – that Charlie was perfectly capable of attending to him in the first instance since there appeared to be nothing seriously wrong with him. But it was a quiet night, and the man – dark-haired and frowning severely – looked the type who might raise a fuss unless his every whim was catered to.

'I see,' said Ewart. 'You do realize, Mr Petherham, that Mr Fairhead here is a fully qualified nurse who is in charge of the staff in this department.'

'I wish to speak to a doctor,' Petherham insisted.

'Well, then,' said Ewart, 'what can I do for you?'

Petherham eyed him suspiciously. He stood straight-backed beside the bed, his fists buried in his trouser pockets.

'Are you a doctor?' he asked.

Aside from his white coat, Ewart, a distinguished-looking man with silvery hair, had a stethoscope around his neck and a bleeper clipped to his breast pocket; under the circumstances, he could scarcely have been mistaken for anything else. But he nodded patiently and said, 'I'm the clinical assistant here. What appears to be the trouble?'

Petherham glanced at Charlie. He also wore a white coat, but his tousled hair and relaxed manner obviously suggested to Petherham a casualness of which he disapproved.

'I would prefer to speak to you alone,' he said stiffly.

Ewart turned to Charlie. 'Mr Fairhead? Do you have any objections?'

'None at all,' Charlie replied with the ghost of a smile that suggested, 'You're welcome to him'. And then he departed, pulling the cubicle curtain shut behind him. His footsteps receded down the corridor.

'Now,' said Ewart, 'what exactly is the problem?'

'A matter of some delicacy,' Petherham told him. He was in his forties, with small eyes and a pinched, buttoned-up face. 'One cannot be too careful in my line of work.'

'Oh?' said Ewart with a show of interest. 'What exactly do you do, Mr Petherham?'

'I am an agent for a company that gathers outstanding credit payments. A highly reputable company, I might add.'

'Ah,' said Ewart, mentally translating this as *Debt Collector*.

'I was making a call on one of my clients at ten o'clock this evening – '

'Rather late for you to be working, isn't it? And on a Saturday night?'

'On the contrary, it is often the only time at which I

16

can catch some of my more elusive clients at home. You would not believe the lengths to which some people will go to avoid me.'

Petherham gave a toothy smile, as though sharing a professional joke. I can believe it, Ewart thought, and he had an image of Petherham creeping down garden pathways to peer in through lighted windows. Don't prejudge the man, he told himself.

'This evening,' Petherham went on, 'I called on a family who have proved particularly reluctant to complete their instalments on a new fitted kitchen. I failed to obtain an answer at the front door, even though lights were burning inside the house. So I walked around to the back.'

Petherham paused, as though marshalling the facts so that he could recite them with perfect accuracy. Ewart felt as if he was listening to a policeman's report.

'In order to gain access to the rear garden and the back door of the house, I had to pass through a wooden gate at the side of the house which was secured by a drop latch. As I was doing so, I suddenly heard a growling sound. Then, out of the darkness, a dog came surging towards me, barking fiercely. I attempted to retreat, but unfortunately the gate had swung shut behind me. Before I was able to open it, the animal leapt upon me.'

Petherham stopped talking and stared at Ewart as if the rest of the story was patently obvious.

'And,' said Ewart, 'you were bitten, I presume.'

'Indeed I was. The animal succeeded in snapping at me before I was able to make my retreat through the gate. It was utterly savage – an appalling incident. People who can't control their animals shouldn't be allowed to keep any. I think I shall write to the RSPCA.'

Ewart nodded understandingly. Before he could say

anything, Petherham went on, 'I wish to have the wound thoroughly attended to so that there is no possibility of infection.'

'Where exactly were you bitten?'

Petherham drew in air, like a sigh in reverse. 'In the fleshy part of my anatomy at the rear.'

'I see,' said Ewart, managing to keep a straight face. 'Would you mind dropping your trousers so that I can inspect the wound.'

Somewhat sheepishly, Petherham complied, hoisting up his coat. Peering closely, Ewart was able to make out a slight abrasion on his left buttock, no more than an inch across.

'Ah yes,' he said, 'the dog's just taken off a few layers of skin. Nothing serious, but you were wise to have it examined. Have you had a course of tetanus injections within the last five years?'

'No, it was longer ago than that.'

'Then we'll give you a booster.'

'Are my trousers damaged?'

Ewart raised them from around Petherham's ankles and examined the seat.

'Not as far as I can see. If you'll excuse me for a few moments.'

He left the cubicle and went down the corridor to the nurses' station. Charlie was there.

'Tetanus?' he said.

'How did you guess?'

'He was muttering something about a savage encounter with a dog while pursuing his line of work. Primary or secondary inoculation?'

'Secondary.'

Charlie nodded triumphantly and produced a hypodermic already prepared. 'Bitten in the bum, was he?'

18

'My lips are sealed,' Ewart said, taking the hypodermic from him. But he couldn't resist a smile as he returned to the cubicle.

Petherham was still standing as he had left him, with his jacket hitched up and his trousers in a pool around his feet.

'This is most embarrassing,' he murmured as Ewart swabbed his buttock preparatory to giving him the injection. 'A most undignified thing to have happened.'

'I shouldn't worry about it too much,' Ewart told him. 'We see all sorts of cases here. Had a young lad in last week whose bottom was stuck to a wooden lavatory seat. His mother brought him in, seat and all. Took three of us to prise it off.'

He was attempting to put Petherham at his ease, but the debt collector remained stiff, tense.

'Right, then,' said Ewart, 'this won't hurt much.'

He slid the needle in.

Petherham gave a tiny whimper which immediately aroused Ewart's sympathy.

'Big dog, was it?' he asked, envisaging an Alsatian or an Irish wolfhound.

'Actually,' said Petherham, 'it was a poodle.'

At that moment, Nurse Simpson opened the door.

'Excuse me, Mr Plimmer,' she said, 'but an RTA's just come in.'

Ewart removed the needle from Petherham's buttock and swabbed the skin.

'Be with you in a moment,' he told her as Petherham hastily pulled up his underpants and trousers.

'You should be fine now,' Ewart told him. 'But if you feel at all unwell in the morning, then visit your GP.'

'I certainly shall.' He buttoned up his coat. 'What precisely is an RTA, if you don't mind me asking?'

19

'A road traffic accident,' Ewart told him.

The girl lay on the bed in the Crash Room, pale and comatose. Ewart was the only doctor on duty that evening, the junior having phoned in earlier to say that she was sick with 'flu. They were also two nurses short, and it was just as well that no other patients had come in during the past hour. The girl was requiring all his attention.

He had examined her thoroughly on her arrival. Two lower ribs had been broken, and there was external bruising of the abdomen. Ewart had had half-hourly girth measurements done on her to check for internal bleeding. She had not regained consciousness since she had been brought in over an hour ago. And her blood pressure had started to fall while her pulse-rate rose.

A peritoneal lavage had revealed that there was free blood in the peritoneal cavity.

'What do your reckon?' Charlie Fairhead asked him.

'I think she may be in danger of a ruptured spleen,' he said. 'Looks like we'll have to operate.'

'Aneasthesia could be tricky,' Charlie said.

Ewart nodded; it almost always was when a patient was already unconscious.

'You sure she's got no identification on her?' he asked.

Charlie nodded. 'We've been through all her clothing. There's nothing.'

'Well, we'd better get her ready for surgery. And I'll give Voyce a call so that he knows exactly what's going on.'

'Is that necessary?'

'Since this is an emergency, strictly speaking it isn't. But it'll make life a little easier for me if Voyce has his feathers stroked, particularly since the girl has no identification.'

He left the bedside and went to the phone in the nurses' station. Voyce's home number was listed in the telephone book, and he dialled it quickly.

The phone began ringing at the other end of the line, and then he heard someone say, 'Good evening, Mr and Mrs Giles Voyce's residence.'

He recognized the French accent of the Voyces' maid, Françoise, whom he had met once at a very stiff social evening at his administrator's home.

'Hello, Françoise,' he said. 'This is Mr Plimmer, calling from the City Hospital. Is Dr Voyce there?'

'I am sorry, Mr Plimmer, but he is not. He and his wife, they have gone out for the evening, to the Adelphi.'

The Adelphi was Holby's premier theatre, an elegant Regency building in the centre of town.

'This is a new production of *A Streetcar Named Desire*,' Françoise was telling him. 'It opened tonight.'

Voyce had always been a theatre buff, and he seldom missed a new production.

'Do you have the theatre's number?' he asked. 'It's important that I contact him.'

'Just one moment.'

There was a silence at the other end of the line, and a long time seemed to pass before Françoise returned to the phone and recited the number to him.

He thanked her rang off, then immediately dialled the Adelphi. A man with a refined and bored-sounding voice answered.

'Hello,' said Ewart. 'Could you tell me if tonight's performance of the Tennessee Williams play has ended yet?'

'The start was delayed by half an hour,' the man informed him.

'I see. And what time do you expect it to finish?'

'Not before midnight.'

21

The wall-clock showed eleven-twenty-four.

'I wonder,' said Ewart, 'if you could pass on a message to one of your audience, a Giles Voyce.'

'That's impossible. We have no public address system here.'

'My name is Ewart Plimmer, and I'm calling from the Casualty Department of Holby City Hospital. Mr Voyce is the hospital administrator, and I'd like him to call me here as soon as possible. Perhaps a message could be left for him when he comes out.'

Ewart heard the man sigh heavily. 'This is most inconvenient. We're very busy here – '

'So are we.' Ewart said. 'And this is important.'

Reluctantly the man made a note of the telephone number and agreed to pass on the message if possible. Ewart put the receiver down, feeling as if he had been on the phone for ages. It was time to get on with the operation, but suddenly Nurse Simpson came hurrying down the corridor.

'I think you'd better come quickly,' she said. 'The girl's heart has stopped.'

1

Ros Plimmer stood in her living room, absently stroking her greying hair and staring out over the immaculate front garden. She was an attractive woman in her early fifties, an ex-headmistress who had retired only two years previously. The garden boasted sculpted flowerbeds, rose bushes in luxuriant bloom, and a lawn that was a perfect, uniform green. A faint smile appeared on her lips, the pleasure of someone who has finally seen all her labours come to fruition. She worked hard on the garden all the year round, and she was particularly pleased with the hollyhocks which were flowering beside the gate.

And yet her eyes remained anxious, watchful, as she gazed out the window. The neo-Georgian house stood in a quiet residential area of the Goldcliff suburb, a few miles north-east of Holby. She and Ewart had bought the place over twenty years ago, when they had still been young and filled with boundless hope for the future. But in the past several weeks, everything had turned sour.

The telephone on the occasional table rang, and she rushed across the room to snatch up the receiver, convinced that it would be Ewart with news of the verdict.

'Ros?' said a female voice. 'Is that you?'

'Oh, hello, Joyce.' She was unable to keep the disappointment out of her voice that it was only her near neighbour.

'Any news?'

'No. Not yet.'

'Are you coping?'

'Just about.'

'Good. Do let us know what happens – especially if it's good news. We're all concerned, you know.'

'Yes. I will.'

She hung up and immediately returned her gaze to the window. She couldn't quite decide whether Joyce really was concerned or simply nosy – the prurient nosiness of neighbours who relished a whiff of scandal. And that whiff had been strong in the air during the past few weeks, attracting curiosity like flies to a carcass.

No. That was unfair. Joyce had been a good friend to them, and it was only natural that she would want to be informed.

She wandered about the house, searching for something to occupy her hands and mind. But the entire place had been thoroughly cleaned and dusted several times in the past month. All the washing and ironing was done, too, buttons sewn on, cupboards emptied out and tidied. She'd even done handiwork such as changing fuses and mending hinges – jobs which Ewart was normally quick to undertake. He'd been unable to function since the case had been brought against him.

Her daughter, Sarah, was lying on a sunbed on the patio at the rear of the house. She wore a skimpy black bikini, her limbs browning in the sun. Her eyes were closed under her white sunhat, and a paperback novel – *Christine* by Stephen King – was draped over her midriff. As an ex-English mistress, Ros did not exactly approve of her choice of reading matter, but she had never been able to interest her in Jane Austen or George Eliot. In a way, this was symptomatic of their whole relationship – they had so little in common.

Ros studied her daughter for a while from the open back door. She looked as if she was dozing, blissfully unconcerned about what was happening to her father. This thought began to make Ros feel annoyed.

'Any news from dad?' Sarah asked abruptly.

She had not opened her eyes or moved, and Ros was taken by surprise.

'No,' she said. 'Nothing yet.'

'It'll be all right.'

'How can you say that? You have no means of knowing.'

'It's just a feeling I have. You'll see.'

Somehow this only added to Ros's irritation.

'I wish I could be as blithe about it as you,' she said.

'I'm not blithe. I just think it's going to be OK.'

Ros had walked outside, and now she was standing over Sarah.

'You shouldn't be reading that rubbish,' she said.

'What rubbish?'

'That book.'

Only now did Sarah open her eyes. She glanced down at the paperback.

'I'm not reading it. Not at this very moment.'

'You know what I mean.'

'Have you ever tried Stephen King?'

'I've no wish to, judging by the cover of his book.'

Sarah made no reply to this, and Ros felt herself bristling even more. There was no proper communication between them – they couldn't even have a decent argument.

'I think the telephone's ringing,' Sarah said.

And it was. Ros rushed inside and once again snatched up the receiver. 'Hello?'

'Ros? Is that you?'

The voice was faint and crackly, but she recognized the faint New Zealand accent of her brother, Gerald. He was an engineer who had emigrated with his family twenty-five years ago and now ran a successful company in Auckland.

'We got your letter,' Gerald was saying. 'What's going on?'

She had written to him a few weeks ago, telling him about Ewart's troubles. But now she could not remember exactly what she had put in the letter.

'He's being sued,' she said.

'Sued?'

'By the parents of the girl who died after the accident. For not operating in time to save her life.'

'But you said in your letter that the girl died before the operation could go ahead.'

That's true, but his administrator seems to feel that he was being over cautious. He's had no support. The coroner's verdict casted doubt on his diagnosis, so the parents decided to sue the Area Health Authority. And Ewart himself.'

She had been over the story so many times she could recite it in her sleep. She had accompanied Ewart to the Coroner's court, and that had proved a real ordeal, with the girl's father shouting at him that he was an incompetent and a murderer. Meanwhile Voyce had offered him no support whatsoever.

'So what happens now?' Gerald asked.

'The case has been heard in the Crown Court. They should have given a verdict by now. I'm expecting to hear from Ewart at any time.'

He picked up the hint. 'Then I'd better get off the phone, hadn't I? Give him our very best. And don't worry. He's a good man, and I'm sure everything will work out fine.'

'That's what Sarah says.'

'And how is she?'

They spent a few seconds ritually enquiring after the state of health of their respective members of family. Then her brother rang off after getting her to promise that she'd call him with news of the verdict. She had seen him only half a dozen times in the last twenty-five years, but they telephoned one another every few months and had remained close. When he hung up, she felt a keen and unexpected sense of abandonment, as if she was suddenly all alone in the world.

She thought she saw a dusty footprint on the Chinese carpet at the centre of the room. The vacuum cleaner would soon shift it.

She heard Ewart's BMW turn into the driveway while she was cleaning crusted grass from the lawnmower hopper in the back garden. Sarah had left earlier to visit a friend who lived nearby – yet another display of her insensitivity – and she decided to try to tidy up the wilderness that was supposed to be Ewart's vegetable garden.

She hurried through the house and entered the hallway just in time to see his blurred outline through the frosted glass panel in the front door. Something made her stop in her tracks, and she waited silently as Ewart's key scratched in the lock.

The door opened, and he entered. He wore a heavy overcoat over his suit, even though the weather was sunny and warm. On seeing her, he gave a thin smile.

'Well?' she said. 'How did it go?'

'At least it's over at last,' he replied.

He said nothing further immediately, but removed his overcoat and hung it on the stand beside the door.

'What was the verdict?' she asked him.

'Not guilty.'

She flung herself into his arms and kissed him.

'Ewart, that's marvellous! Why didn't you ring me with the news?'

'I wanted to tell you in person. There's more. I've resigned.'

She drew back slightly, stared at him. He had been through a long and draining ordeal, and yet there were few signs of it on his face. Only his eyes looked really different, and she couldn't exactly say how. Then it came to her: just recently he hardly ever looked at her – or anyone else – directly for more than a second or two.

'Resigned,' she echoed, utterly at a loss at what to say.

'Well, not officially. Officially I've retired. Retired in disgust.'

'So you'll get your pension.'

He eyed her strangely. 'Oh, yes, they'll look after me financially.'

She followed him through into the living room. He went to the drinks cabinet and mixed himself a gin and tonic, using plenty of gin.

'Want one?' he asked.

'We should be drinking champagne,' she said, at the same time knowing how foolish this sounded. Neither she nor he were in a celebratory mood.

In the kitchen he took two cubes of ice from the freezer and dropped them in his glass. She stood in the doorway, her hand on the lintel, waiting for him to give her a conversational lead. He was like a stranger.

'Tell me what happened,' she said finally.

'There's not a lot to tell. It was simply decided that I was not responsible for the girl's death, so the verdict was not guilty. I bumped into the father outside the court afterwards. He called me a bastard and said it had been fixed.'

'He had no right to say that.'

'Maybe not. But he had every right to be upset.'

'You mustn't let it get to you. You mustn't feel guilty.'

'I don't. We couldn't have moved any faster than we did, but of course intention is no good in this sort of situation if the patient dies on you first. No, what bothers me is the lack of support I got from Voyce and the higher-ups. Everyone back-pedalled. Voyce went on about how he expects his people to use their initiative, while in practice he's doing everything in his power to stifle it. The hypocrisy of the man – it's sickening.'

He took a large gulp of his drink. Ros became aware that her knuckles were white around the edge of the lintel.

'The only support I got was from the staff. Charlie Fairhead and the two nurses backed me, but that was all. I could hardly believe it.

'Well, you've given them the best years of your life. You're better off out of it.'

'Maybe. Maybe.'

'Let's go and sit down.'

'I need another drink first.'

Ros perched herself on the edge of the armchair beside the window while Ewart made himself another gin and tonic. She felt tense, apprehensive in some vague but profound way.

'You sure you don't want one?' Ewart asked.

'I'll have the same as you.'

He mixed the drink equally strong for her, and she gulped at it gratefully. Somewhere outside a blackbird was chirping, its lyrical song totally at odds with the strained atmosphere inside.

Ewart had finally sat down opposite her, but he was staring out the window. The fingers of his left hand were drumming out a slow rhythm on the arm of his chair, and she wondered what music was playing in his head. Classical records were one of his few passions outside medicine.

She decided to take a firm approach.

'Listen,' she said to him, 'you're fifty-five, and you've spent twenty years working for the health service. You've done your stint. I took an early retirement because I wanted to enjoy life, and now you can do the same.'

'It's left a nasty taste in my mouth. I'm not sure I have the appetite for anything else.'

'Not at the moment, perhaps. But that feeling will pass.'

He glanced briefly at her as if he was not convinced, then returned to staring through the window. The blackbird was still in full song.

'Now we have the opportunity to spend some time together,' she went on. 'It's not easy being a doctor's wife, you know. I've seen very little of you since you became a surgeon. Now we can do more things together.'

'Yes,' he said, brightening a little. 'You're right.'

'We can have a proper holiday for a start. We've been promising ourselves one for years.'

At that moment, the door opened and in walked Sarah.

'Hello, dad,' she said. 'I was watching out for your car, but I thought I'd give you and mum a few minutes alone together. How did it go?'

'Not guilty,' Ros told her before Ewart could say anything. 'It's disgraceful what he had to go through.'

Sarah kept her eyes on her father. 'That's great news, dad!'

Ewart nodded and gave a thin smile. Sarah pecked him on the forehead.

'Your father's decided to retire,' Ros told her.

Sarah peered at him. He nodded again.

'I always thought you'd keep going until you dropped,' she said to him. 'Married to your work, and all that. What are you going to do with your free time?'

'Your father and I are going to take a holiday soon,' Ros said.

'Oh, goodie – I'll have the house to myself.'

'It's time you found yourself a job, young lady. If I'd had my way you'd have never been allowed to leave school.'

This was an argument which had been going on for over a year, and Sarah clearly was not going to rise to it.

'Cup of tea, anyone?' she said brightly. 'Or shall I fill up your glasses again?'

Ewart sat in bed, desperately trying to concentrate on the copy of *Oliver Twist* which he was holding. It was one of the many books he had always been meaning to read but had never actually got around to. And now his mind kept wandering so that he was scanning whole paragraphs without absorbing a word.

Water was running in the bathroom as Ros performed her ablutions. Ewart made another attempt to give Dickens the attention he deserved, but it was no use; his thoughts were still distracted.

He kept returning to the ordeals of the Coroner's Court and then the Crown Court, running the details over and over in his head, and to no great purpose. In the end he had been vindicated, but the experience had somehow eroded his faith in himself so that he was unable to carry on. Retirement had seemed not simply the honourable option but an essential one – he felt as if he could no longer function.

He put the book aside and lay back, staring up at the ceiling. What was he going to do now? Catch up on half a lifetime's reading? Take up woodworking or origami? Spend eighteen hours a day listening to music? Actually get around to digging over the back garden and planting a few peas and potatoes? None of these ideas held any great appeal.

The bathroom door opened and Ros emerged in her nightgown. She wore a frilly floral bathcap over her hair, tufted slippers on her feet. He caught a whiff of musk as she climbed in beside him.

'What happened to *Oliver Twist*?' she asked him.

'We weren't communicating,' he replied. 'Maybe another time.'

'Sleepy?'

'Not particularly.'

'Then I've got something to show you.'

She reached down and opened one of the drawers of the cabinet on her side of the bed.

'Holidays,' she said, plumping down a pile of brochures between them. 'I got them while I was out shopping this afternoon.'

'Good grief, there's half a library here.'

'Twenty-six actually. I thought it would be useful to have as much choice as possible.'

She thumbed through them and selected one. 'How do you feel about Jamaica?'

'Never met her.'

'Be serious, Ewart. We both need a good break. Or there's Morocco, Yugoslavia, Greece – you name it.'

'Greenland?'

She gave him a patient smile. 'If we can get the bookings, there's nothing to stop us from going as soon as we can. Is there?'

'I suppose not.'

'You remember the last holiday we had?'

Ewart started to think, but she quickly filled in the blank:

'A long weekend in Brighton, in 1982. That's four years ago, Ewart. This time we're going to have a proper holiday – a fortnight in the sun. I don't care where it is, as long as it's not in this country.'

Ewart spent the next half hour gazing at glossy pictures of people basking on white Caribbean beaches, or gazing from boats at Greek islands in radiant blue seas, or having cocktails on patios of elegant hotels in Sicily, Spain and the South of France.

'Well,' Ros said at length, 'what do you think?'

'Very nice.'

She sighed. 'Which do you prefer, Ewart? Jamaica, Portugal or Crete? They're the three that look most interesting to me.'

He glanced again at the brochures which were spread out all over the bed. His mind was blank.

'I couldn't really say.'

'You must have a preference. Or would you just like me to decide?'

It was his turn to sigh. 'Ros, I don't think I'm really ready for this.'

'What do you mean?'

'For choosing a holiday, or for going anywhere straightaway.'

'I don't understand. Why not?'

'I need a bit of time to myself, to take stock.'

'You also need a holiday. I do, too.'

'I know. Don't think I'm not grateful for your support over the past couple of months – '

'You should have let me come with you for the verdict.'

'No, you'd been through enough, we agreed that.'

'It might have helped.'

'We got the result we wanted, didn't we? It's all over now.'

'So what's the problem?'

She looked anxious, disappointed, and he found it hard to meet her eyes.

'I just need a little time to decide what I'm going to do with the rest of my life.'

2

'How much longer are you going to be in there?' Charlie Fairhead shouted through the bathroom door.

There was no immediate reply.

'Liz', he called. 'Haven't drowned in there, have you?'

'I'm putting on my make-up,' she replied in the steady tones of someone engaged in a delicate task.

'You've been in there almost an hour. My bladder's crying out for relief.'

'Won't be a moment.'

'That's what you said ten minutes ago.'

'That's the trouble with men – they have no patience.'

'And you know the trouble with women? They don't even know the meaning of the word.'

'Just go away and let me finish.'

Charlie wandered off, going into the kitchen. The remains of his breakfast still sat on the table, even though it was almost noon – bacon rinds, egg yolk, baked bean juice and the crusts of fried bread. Thoroughly unhealthy, but he loved it, always had. He'd been working the afternoon shift at the hospital and had not got up until eleven.

He took a cigarette from the packet of Benson & Hedges on the table and lit up, exhaling smoke through his nose. The bathroom door opened and Liz emerged. Charlie hurried past her, kicking the bathroom door shut behind him.

Only when he emerged did he notice the care which

Liz had put into getting dressed. She worked as a pre-
senter for a local radio station, doing a music-cum-
current-affairs programme which ran on the afternoon
slot from two till six Mondays to Saturdays. Normally she
was content to go into work in a jeans and sweater, but
today she was wearing her best charcoal-grey suit with a
cream blouse and a striped tie loosely knotted at her
neck. She had made herself up very painstakingly, and
the effect was elegant and alluring.

'What's up?' he asked. 'You meeting royalty?'

'We've got a guy coming down from London to watch
our operation for a few days. Nick said he wanted all of
us on our best behaviour and in our best bib and tucker.'

Nick was the station boss, a talkative, go-ahead man
whom Charlie had never really taken to.

'A sponsor?' he said.

'Could be, if we impress him sufficiently.'

She smiled, her teeth pure white against the cherry-red
of her lipstick. 'I did tell you about it the other day, but I
think you must have fallen asleep.'

'It's the afternoon shift – plays hell with my body-
clock. Give me straight nights any day. I don't even know
what day it is.'

'It's Monday – and I'd better be going.'

'Hang on a minute,' he said, taking her by the arm.
'It's been a while since I've seen you in a skirt.'

He eyed her appreciatively. She was an attractive
blonde in her late twenties, and they had met not long
after Charlie had moved to Holby. Soon after that, they
had decided to live together and had found a first-floor
flat in a Victorian house which was conveniently close to
the city centre for both of them. Their working patterns
rarely coincided so that they had few mutual friends and
precious little social life. But what they got up to when

they were in bed together was ample compensation for that.

'Black stockings, too,' Charlie said, giving her a leer. 'How about sparing me a quick half-hour?'

She pulled away from him. 'It's no good getting fruity – I've got to go.'

'Ten minutes, then.'

'No chance.'

'What if I insist?'

She began to back away, pretending to be afraid. But he could see the playfulness in her eyes. He darted forward, and she bolted for the bedroom, attempting to slam the door. But he jammed his foot in the gap, preventing her from closing it.

'Get out of here, you maniac!' she said as he began to force the door open. But she was grinning at the same time.

He got his body through the gap, then grabbed her, picking her up and carrying her towards the bed. Just before he threw her down on the mattress, she said, 'All right, I give in. But if you crease my skirt, I'll murder you!'

Ros Plimmer was eating a belated lunch of cold chicken and coleslaw when the telephone rang. She put the plate aside and went into the living room.

'Ros Plimmer speaking,' she said into the mouthpiece.

'Mrs Plimmer, this is Charlie Fairhead.'

'Ah. Good afternoon, Mr Fairhead.'

'Is Ewart there, by any chance?'

'I'm afraid not. He went out earlier.'

'Did you leave him my message?'

'Yes, Mr Fairhead. I told him you phoned yesterday,

and the day before. I'm afraid he doesn't want to speak to you. He doesn't want to speak to *anyone*.'

Silence fell for a moment.

'Do you have any idea where he might have gone?'

'I have a suspicion.'

'Would you mind telling me? It's quite important that I talk to him.'

'Yes, I would mind, Mr Fairhead. If my husband doesn't wish to be disturbed, then that's his business.'

Again there was a pause.

'I see. Well, thank you anyway, Mrs Plimmer.'

He hung up.

Ros put the receiver down and wandered back into the kitchen. Half her lunch remained uneaten on the plate, but she had lost her appetite for it.

Two weeks had passed since the Crown Court verdict – two weeks in which Ewart had become withdrawn and reclusive. He refused to speak to anyone outside the immediate family – even Gerald, who had rung twice from Auckland to try to talk to him. She had tried to be sympathetic at first, had deferred to his moods in the hope that he would revert to his old self. But as the days had passed and there had been no change in his behaviour – if anything, he was getting worse – she had found her sympathy in shorter and shorter supply.

Earlier she'd had an argument with Sarah over some trifling matter, and the girl was now huddled in her bedroom behind a locked door, refusing to come out. She knew that because she was having difficulty in communicating with Ewart, Sarah was suffering the brunt of her anxiety. She was turning into a nag. And more than ever, she felt as if she was alone in the house twenty-four hours a day.

The phone call had rattled her more than she'd

expected, even though she had tried to remain icily polite. She had no personal grudge against Charlie Fairhead, but she didn't want him phoning the house every day, wanting Ewart. She felt sure it would be something to do with hospital work, and she wanted her husband to put all that firmly in his past. Otherwise it was hard to see what sort of future lay ahead for the two of them.

Almost unconsciously she had wandered into the living room and was pouring herself a sherry. She stopped, then tipped the drink back into the bottle before corking it.

One drinker in the family's enough, she thought as she rinsed out the glass in the kitchen, then dried it with a tea-towel. Ewart had not been rising until late in the morning, and most days he left soon afterwards without eating breakfast, driving off without telling her where he was going. He returned late in the evening, smelling of whisky or gin, and slumped morosely in front of the television, watching it mindlessly until the last programme had finished.

She'd tried talking to him, but that was no good. She'd tried silences and nagging, to no avail. He insisted that nothing was wrong, claimed that he was simply relaxing, following his own impulses for a while. Well, she wasn't going to be able to stand much more of it.

The doorbell chimed, startling her. She crept into the hallway and recognized the blurred outline of her neighbour, Joyce, calling in for a chat, as she had done every other afternoon since the verdict. Ewart avoided her like the plague.

Charlie's car was a battered old Ford Cortina estate, its fading puce colour helping to hide the rust spots which were blossoming like acne over the bodywork. A tape of

39

Janis Joplin singing 'Ball and Chain' was playing as he drove through the centre of Holby, puffing on a cigarette; he had been a fan of hers since the sixties.

He had missed the lunch-hour rush, and the traffic was light along Avon Street, the main road through the centre of the city. Holby was a place into which he had fitted well, and he thought of it as a kind of compressed version of London without all the nasty bits. Well, without most of them: it had its ghettos and wastelands like any other big place. A city of a quarter of a million inhabitants, it lay on the River Holby, only a few miles from the Bristol Channel. The Severn Bridge to the north-east gave access to South Wales, and a motorway ran from the outskirts of the city right across the country to London. He could reach his mum and dad's place in Ealing in just over an hour's driving on a good day.

Charlie turned down a sidestreet, taking a short cut on to another main road. He had finally managed to track down Ewart Plimmer after several days of trying. When his wife had mentioned that he had been going out every afternoon, Charlie had remembered Ewart mentioning a snooker club called Renfrew's where he sometimes took a few drinks after work. The old bod who'd answered his telephone call to the club had refused to confirm that Ewart was actually in attendance that afternoon; but he had let slip that it had been a regular watering-hole of his in recent weeks.

Charlie was dressed in faded Levi's and a baggy white T-shirt over a battered brown leather jacket. He was well aware that Renfrew's was not your average working men's pool hall but a fairly refined club. There was even a doorman on duty outside the white-painted Regency facade. He could not disguise his surprise as Charlie pulled into a parking space near the entrance and climbed out.

'Excuse me, sir,' he said as Charlie climbed the steps towards him, 'but that parking space is reserved for members.'

'And guests?' Charlie suggested.

'Well, yes – '

'I'm here on Ewart Plimmer's invitation,' he said, sweeping past the man before he could say anything further.

Inside the lobby was furnished with a burgundy carpet and mahogany and brass fittings. A door with a pointed Gothic revival arch led into the main part of the club.

Outside it was a bright, sunny day, but in the pool room an artificial twilight prevailed. Heavy curtains had been drawn on all the windows, and the only illumination apart from the discreetly lit bar was the cones of light over the three snooker tables at the centre of the room.

Only one table was being used, two elderly men prodding balls around the green baize. Sumptuous chairs of padded chestnut leather lined the walls and surrounded low tables of dark gleaming wood. The place smelt of cowhide and old cigars.

Charlie did a slow circuit of the room, peering at the faces in the chairs. Most were plump and elderly – ex-colonels, he imagined, or barristers or retired bank managers. One or two of them stared at him with obvious disapproval as he passed by; his jeans and leather jacket were blatantly out of place in such well-heeled surroundings. Charlie enjoyed getting this reaction since he basically disapproved of any institution that smacked of exclusivity and conspicuous affluence.

At last he spotted Ewart sitting alone in an armchair in the far corner of the room, close to the bar. A drink sat on the table in front of him – scotch, Charlie guessed – and there was a folded newspaper on his lap. He sat with his hands folded, staring into space, and did not notice Charlie as he approached.

'Good afternoon, Ewart.'

'Eh?' Ewart looked up.

'Nice place you've got here.'

'Charlie. What are you doing here?'

Charlie took a seat opposite him. 'More to the point, what are *you* doing here?'

Ewart picked up his drink and took a sip of it. 'Getting away from it all.'

'So I gathered. I've been ringing you for days, trying to talk to you.'

Ewart shrugged. 'Nothing personal, Charlie. I haven't felt in the mood for talking to anyone.'

'Still bruised over the girl who died, eh?'

Ewart said nothing.

'Long time to be in mourning, isn't it? Especially for a doctor.'

'I'm not a doctor any more, Charlie. I've retired.'

'Yes. But the principle's the same.'

Ewart sighed, not looking at him. He took another mouthful of his drink. 'It wasn't really the girl dying, but what happened afterwards. The whole farrago.'

'Yeah, it was a bloody farce, especially with Voyce being so two-faced. Did you know he's gone?'

'Gone?'

'Resigned. Become part of the brain-drain. Got a job in Florida, in a hospital for rich geriatrics. Good riddance to him, I say.'

'He didn't give any inkling of it during the trials.'

'No, well he wouldn't, would you? Always a slippery customer, our Dr Voyce.'

'Who's his replacement?'

'Norman Parker. You know him, don't you?'

'Slightly. I'll tell you something – he's a better man than Voyce. Firm but fair.'

'That might not stop him closing down the Casualty Department at the City Hospital.'

'What?'

'There's talk that they're planning on centralizing the facilities, and this could mean that the department will be shut down.'

'But that's ridiculous. It's needed.'

'I couldn't agree more. But of course I haven't really got the clout to argue the case.'

Ewart looked at him, and Charlie could see that he had finally realized what he was leading up to – or at least part of it.

'Now wait a minute, Charlie – '

'How about a drink? I could use a bit of lubrication.'

Ewart smiled slowly. 'What'll you have?'

'A pint of bitter would go down nicely – if they serve it in this sort of place.'

'They do. It's not as bad as it looks, Charlie. They do a lot of work for charity here – fêtes and sports meetings, that sort of thing.'

'I'm pleased to hear it. I thought perhaps you were turning into a bit of a reactionary in your old age.'

'Not with young radicals like you around to keep me on my toes.'

'Oh, I wouldn't call myself a radical. Just a concerned citizen – concerned for the people who are least able to defend themselves in this society of ours. People like casualty victims.'

Ewart had risen and was rummaging in his pocket for cash. Charlie had always respected him as one of the few men who had yet to succumb to the pressures of the system – pressures which sometimes forced doctors to forget their idealism and take the least line of resistance. Ewart had always stood up for what he believed in, and it bothered Charlie to see him looking so listless and defeated.

'If anyone should ask you,' Charlie said to Ewart, 'I told the doorman I'm here as your guest.'

'Cheeky,' said Ewart.

'I don't mind wearing a tie if I have to. But I haven't brought one with me, and I can't do anything about my jeans.'

'You're incorrigible.'

'So people keep telling me. I'm still not sure what it means.'

'So when are they planning on closing the department?' Ewart asked Charlie.

'We don't know that they are for sure. At the moment it's just a rumour. But you know how often rumours turn into reality.'

'It would be madness to centralize. The department is barely able to cope with the workload as it is.'

'Too royal. And we get a lot of trainees thrust on us, thrown in at the deep end. What we need is a solid nucleus of trained and committed staff, particularly on the night shift.'

Ewart took a mouthful of scotch, agreeing with Charlie but not wanting to commit himself too strongly. He had a feeling that Charlie was working around to some proposition, but he remained firm in his resolve that he'd finished with medicine.

'Fancy another one?' Charlie said, holding up his empty pint glass.

'That hardly touched the sides.'

'It's my day off. Nothing like a few beers to help you wind down.'

Ewart drained his glass and offered it to Charlie.

'You'll have no problems getting served,' he said. 'I told the barman you were the wayward youngest son of the Earl of Everley.'

'Never heard of him,' Charlie said.

'Neither have I. But the barman was impressed.'

'If I'm incorrigible, then you're an old rogue.'

Charlie went off to the bar, leaving Ewart to ruminate over what he had said. The cuts which the DHSS and the regional health authorities were forcing hospitals to make were having a gravely damaging effect on the health services. Ewart was a Welshman who had been born in the mining town of Tredegar, where Aneurin Bevan had initiated a prototype of the National Health System by deducting a small amount of money from miners' wages each week in exchange for free medical treatment. And in 1948 the system had been introduced nationwide, providing cover for millions of ordinary people. But now, in 1986, the idealism and compassion which had lain behind the NHS was dying, its infrastructure eroded by harsh economic doctrines which seemed to demand that the caring services be run on the cost-efficient basis of some slick multinational company.

Ewart was no socialist – he was too much of a maverick ever to follow one party line – but he did believe that the underprivileged had to be looked after by society as a whole, and that meant government support for a nation-wide system of health care. He had not lived in Wales since his student days, but as a small boy he remembered his father, a winder at a local colliery, having an accident which might have resulted in the amputation of his hand

45

had not medical treatment been immediately available — and affordable.

'There you go,' said Charlie, returning with his drink.

They sat in silence for a while, listening to the almost subliminal murmur of conversation and the occasional clack of billiard balls.

Charlie said, 'Not much action here, is there?'

'That's why I like it,' Ewart replied. 'It's a complete contrast to hospital life.'

'I bet you miss it, though.'

'What?'

'The hospital.'

'No, I've finished with it now.'

But there was a lack of conviction in his voice which even he recognized.

The second of the three tables was now occupied by two middle-aged men who were playing snooker.

'You any good at that?' Charlie asked.

'Passable,' Ewart told him.

'That's not what I hear. Won a regional hospital competition a few years back, didn't you?'

'You must have spies everywhere.'

'I just like to keep my ears open. I'm quite handy with a cue myself. Fancy a game? I reckon I could take you.'

'All right, you're on.'

They crossed to the rack beside the door and selected a cue each.

'What's your game?' Ewart asked. 'Billiards or snooker?'

'I prefer snooker. More balls to hit.'

'Snooker it is, then.'

'How about best of three games?'

'Fine,' said Ewart. But his glass was empty, and so, too, was Charlie's.

'You set them up,' he told the younger man. 'I'll get us some more drinks.'

Ewart peered down the length of his cue, lining up the black. If he potted it, he won the frame. The black was close to the edge of the pocket, but the white ball was at the other end of the table, tight against the cushion.

Ewart steadied himself and murmured, 'Here goes everything.' Then he hit the cue ball softly but firmly.

The ball rolled down the table and nudged the black. It trickled towards the pocket, hovered, then dropped.

'Good shot,' said Charlie. 'That makes it five frames all.'

Ewart straightened and immediately noticed that both their glasses were empty on the table nearby. 'Whose round is it?'

'Mine,' said Charlie.

Ewart set up the balls while Charlie was at the bar. His wristwatch showed that it was after six. He felt as if they had only been playing for an hour or so, but the whole afternoon had passed. They had both been drinking steadily and were now in a controlled state of tipsiness. At least I hope it's controlled, Ewart thought, knowing that he would have to get a taxi home.

Charlie returned with the drinks, setting them down on the table.

'Your break,' Ewart reminded him.

Charlie picked up his cue and began chalking the tip.

'At least you're sounding a bit more cheerful now,' he said to Ewart. 'When I walked in here, you looked as miserable as sin.'

'After what happened,' Ewart said, 'how did you expect me to be? Jumping with joy?'

'Well, if you'd been angry I could have understood it.

Or resentful. Or bitter. But not morose and withdrawn like you've been.'

Charlie had a cigarette in his mouth, and Ewart said, 'You smoke too much, you know.'

'Don't try and change the subject.'

'You're a bit young to be giving me a pep-talk.'

'Someone has to.'

'Just break, will you?'

But Charlie made no move to do so. 'You know what I think?'

'No. And I don't want to.'

'I think you're really missing it all. I think you're depressed because you were forced to retire before you felt your job was done. You've got plenty of years' service left in you yet.'

Ewart took a gulp of his drink. He didn't say anything, but he immediately knew that Charlie was right. By suppressing all the bitterness he'd felt at his enforced retirement, he'd merely plunged himself into gloom.

Charlie was waiting for him to say something.

'What difference does it make to you?' he asked.

'It makes a lot of difference, particularly with the department under threat of closure.'

'I don't see what that has to do with me now. There's nothing I can do about it.'

'Maybe there is. If you were willing.'

'Willing? Willing to do what?'

'Go to Norman Parker and present him with a different sort of package.'

'What are you talking about?'

'You've agreed with me that we're usually understaffed on Casualty, right? And that night-time facilities are woefully inadequate, yes?'

Ewart nodded.

'So what we need is to strengthen the department. And what better way than to present Norman Parker with the idea of a *permanent* night-shift, manned seven days a week by staff who are totally committed to the idea?'

Charlie was still chalking his cue, and a cloud of pale blue dust was forming on the green baize of the table. Before Ewart could say anything, he went on: 'It's not just a bit of political manoeuvring to save the department, Ewart – I really believe in the idea. You know as well as I do that the department isn't giving the public the service it needs. From Sundays to Thursdays it isn't even open between midnight and six, and what use is that to someone who's had a motorway accident or a stroke in the middle of the night. But *because* we're not open, the Area Health Authority can claim that we're not really needed at those times. But if we could get a permanent night shift set up, even on a trial basis, we could prove to them that we're essential. And that might knock on the head the idea of closing down the department.'

Ewart took a sip of his drink, pondering. The idea was a sound one, not simply because of the greater service which would be provided for the public, but because staff could be selected who actually preferred working nights, thus minimizing absenteeism on the shift.

'What do you think?' Charlie prompted him.

'I think you're in danger of wearing away that chalk,' Ewart said.

Charlie put the cube down on the edge of the table and blew on the tip of his cue. Then he crouched over the semi-circle and hit the white ball hard. The triangle of reds burst apart.

'I'm still not sure where I fit into all this,' Ewart said. 'After all, I'm a private citizen now.'

'Not if you offer to come out of retirement to head the department.'

'So that's what you've been leading up to.'

'That's it. With your clout behind the idea, we might be able to swing it with Parker. If he agrees, then I think I can get some really good staff.'

Ewart walked around the table and lined up an easy red. He fluffed the shot.

'It's not just using you as a diplomat,' Charlie said. 'I know how much you believe in the value of permanently staffed Casualty Departments which are open all hours to the public. I also know that you're a bit of a night-bird, just like me. And you need the challenge – you need to be in the front-line. Otherwise you're just going to wither away.'

Charlie potted a red and lined himself up for the black. This, too, he potted. For the next ten minutes or so, Ewart watched as Charlie amassed a match-winning break. He was utterly concentrated on the task. A determined man, with passionate convictions about things and an equally passionate need to make his ideals a reality.

'You're the perfect man for the job,' he said to Ewart. 'What do you say?'

'I feel as if I'm being blackmailed. You've been getting me drunk in the hope that I'll say yes.'

'Of course I have. But there's no one else I'd have approached.'

'I appreciate that.'

'Then you'll give it a crack?'

'I'll think about it.'

Charlie looked a shade disappointed. He indicated the

two men who were playing on the table next to him – both well-heeled and wearing expensive suits.

'Think about this,' he said. 'Those two have probably got private medical insurance so that they can have their in-growing toenails or wisdom teeth removed in some plush BUPA hospital the day after tomorrow if they wanted. But what about the guy who chops his hand up in a machine in the middle of the night, or the old woman who falls down a flight of concrete stairs on some crummy council estate? You won't find any wounded bleeding over the wall-to-wall carpets of private hospitals, will you? Much too messy for the public image.'

Ewart felt a flicker of anger. 'You don't have to lecture me, you know. I've worked for the NHS for twenty years.'

Charlie shrugged. 'I know that, but things are grimmer now than ever. And if people like you back out of the fight, what hope do we have?'

Ewart swallowed the last of his drink. 'All right, damn it – you've persuaded me. I'll see Norman Parker and do my damnedest to sell him on the idea.'

Charlie immediately brightened. 'That's great!' He brandished his empty pint glass. 'One more for the road?'

'No, I'm going home – by taxi. And you shouldn't be driving, either, the amount you've drunk.'

'I'm not going to. I asked the barman if he'd let me get my head down for a few hours in one of your armchairs, and he said yes.'

'You must have impressed him.'

'I have my moments,' Charlie said in a refined accent which he had obviously used to convince the barman that he was indeed the Earl of Everley's youngest son. 'You didn't tell me he was gay.'

'I didn't think it mattered.'

'It doesn't – not theoretically, anyway. But I think he fancies me.'

3

'Where are you going?' Ros Plimmer asked her husband.

'To see someone.'

'Who?'

'I can't talk about it now.'

Ros lay in bed, watching Ewart as he knotted his tie. He had risen early that morning, and had showered and dressed before she had fully emerged from sleep. In the past week – ever since he'd come home very drunk, muttering about bumping into Charlie Fairhead – she had noticed a change in him. But he still refused to tell her what was going on.

'Is it someone at the hospital?' she asked.

'Yes.'

'About a job?'

'It's just a meeting, for a chat.' He rose from the dressing table and came over to her, pecking her on the cheek. 'I'll tell you all about it later, I promise.'

And then he was hurrying towards the door.

Ros sat up in bed and made to say something. But Ewart was already gone, the door closed firmly behind him. A sinking feeling overcame her – a sense that things were slipping out of her grasp. Ewart had that preoccupied, almost animated look in his eyes, but she knew that it had nothing whatsoever to do with her.

'Take a seat,' Norman Parker said, ushering Ewart into his office. He was a tall, dark-haired man of Ewart's age, dressed in a brown hounds'-tooth suit. The lenses of his glasses twinkled in the strip lighting as he sat down at his desk opposite Ewart.

'So,' he said, 'how is retirement treating you?'

'Boring,' Ewart said without hesitation. 'I can't find anything interesting to do to occupy my time.'

'That doesn't surprise me, Ewart. I always thought you'd keep going until you dropped.'

Ewart had known Parker since their student days together in London. Their careers had taken different routes, and they had not seen much of one another in recent years; but there was still an easy familiarity between them.

'I think you're right,' Ewart told him. 'I'd like to be involved in hospital work again.'

'Oh?' said Parker, pretending innocence. 'Anything particular in mind?'

'Of course. Otherwise I wouldn't be here.'

'Ah. So it wasn't a social call after all. Missing poking about inside people's anatomies, eh?'

'Not so much that – I think I'm getting a bit old for a constant diet of blood and guts. But I'd still like to be there in the background, advising and helping a team.'

'And what sort of team exactly?'

'A regular night-shift team on Casualty.'

Parker took a handkerchief from his pocket, removed his glasses and proceeded to polish the lenses.

'I'd heard mutterings that this idea was in the air,' he said presently. 'Do you also know that there's talk of closing down the Casualty Department completely and transferring it to a centralized unit?'

'Yes. And in my view that would be a disastrous move. We *need* the department here, open permanently, seven days a week.'

'You know I'm under pressure to make our services

more efficient. Make better use of manpower, cut out the dead wood.'

'What dead wood, for God's sake? All we're ever hearing these days is talk of efficiency and centralization. What it means in practice is staff cuts and fewer facilities for the public. The NHS isn't a *business*, it's a *service*, and we should be providing what the public needs, irrespective of the cost.'

'Try telling that to health department ministers and senior civil servants.'

'Look, Norman, I know you're up against it – I know you've got these people breathing down your neck, wanting more and more economies. But when's it going to stop? When the National Health Service is economized out of existence?'

Parker, still polishing his glasses, said nothing.

'Someone's got to make a stand,' Ewart went on. 'We have to try to prove to these people that we really do need the services they want to axe.'

'I'd have hardly thought that the Casualty Department is the best place to start with that, and particularly the night shift. Not exactly the easiest place to work, is it? And it's getting slowly worse, with nurses worried about being assaulted by drunken patients or half-mad derelicts.'

'That's precisely why we have to stop the rot there. And that's why we need a permanent staff who are committed to the shift and the work.'

Parker put his glasses back on. 'And you'd be prepared to take charge of the shift?'

Ewart nodded. 'I would. As far as hospitals go, Casualty is in the firing-line. The nurses and doctors there need all the support we can give them. It's where medicine

55

and the real world collide in the most dramatic and vital way.'

'That sounds dangerously like missionary zeal to me.' But Parker smiled as he said it.

'Perhaps it is,' Ewart responded. 'But there's nothing wrong in believing passionately about saving people's lives.'

Parker nodded. 'Indeed not. But would you be prepared to make the necessary financial sacrifice as well? It's one thing to talk about ideals, another thing to stick to them when it's going to affect your pocket. Assuming we did go ahead with the idea of a permanent night-shift staff, would you be prepared to head it on a salary that would only be a fraction of what you've been earning as a clinical assistant?'

'Yes,' Ewart said without hesitation. 'I've been paid well for my work over the past twenty years. Now it's time I gave a little bit back for something I really believe in.'

Parker stared at him, and Ewart felt as if he was being assessed. He said, 'This wasn't my idea originally, you know. Charlie Fairhead came up with it. But it makes such obvious sense.'

'Bit of a firebrand, isn't he? Fairhead?'

Ewart grinned. 'He has his moments. But he's totally committed to his work, and damn good at it, too. I'd want him as Charge Nurse if we get the go-ahead.'

Again Parker was silent, thoughtful.

'Well,' he said at last, 'it may help me swing the idea if you're prepared to come out of retirement for it. A former clinical assistant taking over the running of a night-shift Casualty department. Not something that happens every day.'

'Then you'll back it?'

56

'I think it may be worth a try. But I can't promise you anything in today's political climate.'

'I'd be prepared to take whatever facilities you could offer, as long as we've got sufficient staff.'

'All right, Ewart. I'll see what I can do.'

Ros Plimmer prodded the food on her plate with her fork.

'A permanent night staff?' she said, incredulous. 'And you'd be heading it?'

'That's the idea,' Ewart said through a mouthful of stuffed veal escalopes. 'If Norman Parker can swing it. This is delicious, by the way.'

She had laboured all morning over the lunch, wanting to concoct something special. But now the meal tasted like ashes in her mouth.

'I'd see hardly anything of you,' she said.

'Of course you would. It's not as if I'd be working seven days a week, fifty-two weeks a year.'

'I thought you'd decided to retire so that we could spend more time together.'

'I retired out of disgust,' he told her, another forkful *en route* to his mouth. 'It's not what I wanted to do – you know that.'

'Do I? Do I really? And how in God's name am I supposed to know that?'

Her voice had become raised, angry. For the first time, Ewart looked up at her from his food.

'You never tell me anything,' she said vehemently. 'You never discuss things with me any more. You just decide what you want to do, and then you go ahead and do it, without consulting me.'

He tried to say something, but she cut him off. 'For weeks I've been hanging around this house, tolerating your moods, cooking your meals, letting you come and go as you please. And you haven't given one damn moment of thought for how I might be feeling.'

She could see that he was taken aback by her outburst. But weeks and weeks of pent-up anger could no longer be denied. Her hands were trembling, and she felt shaky inside. But she was determined to say her piece.

He put his cutlery down on his plate and stared at her for long moments without speaking. Then he said, 'You're right. I'm sorry.'

'You're sorry. Is that all you've got to say for yourself?'

He shook his head. 'It's not all, no. I realize that I've been terribly neglectful of you and wrapped up in my own misery. But the thing is, Ros – I can't stop working.'

She was silent.

'I know you were glad when I said I'd retire. I know you were hoping we could now start living the normal life of a retired couple – holidays and all that – '

'Holidays are not so much to ask for.'

'You're right. You're right. But this thing – this business with the permanent night casualty staff – it's important. If I don't do it, no one else will.'

'So it's just public-spiritedness, is it?'

'You know it's not just that. I need to be involved in hospital work somehow. Otherwise I'm not going to be any use at all. They're planning to close down the Casualty Department altogether. But if I can persuade Parker – '

'You just can't bear the thought of having to be here, with me, all day and every day.'

As soon as the words were out, Ros began to wish she hadn't spoken. Ewart was frowning, but she could not read his expression, could not guess what he was thinking.

It's slipping away, she thought. The harder I try to hang on, the faster it's slipping away.

At that moment the dining room door opened and in walked Sarah, dressed in white tennis shorts and a low-cut Gucci T-shirt. With her was her friend, Natalie, a tall, dark-haired girl, similarly attired. With their matching tans and perfect white teeth, they looked to Ros at that moment like a pair of twins.

'Hello, you two,' said Sarah. 'That looks good.'

She was staring down at her father's plate. Ros said, 'I only made enough for the two of us. If you'd told me you and Natalie were coming for lunch – '

'We're not,' Sarah said. 'Actually, we're about to drive into town for a Kentucky fried takeaway.'

Ros made a disapproving noise. 'I don't know how you can eat that rubbish all the time.'

She nodded at Natalie, who was lingering awkwardly in the background, obviously sensing the fraught atmosphere. Like Sarah, she was eighteen and had left school the previous summer. Like her, she was still unemployed though well provided for by her father, a bank manager. Ros had always found her polite and affable – a reliable sort, and therefore difficult to disapprove of.

'Natalie and I were thinking of taking a holiday,' Sarah remarked.

'Oh?' said Ros.

'With Stephanie and Ruth. We were thinking of going grape-picking in the South of France. Apparently the money's quite good, and you get plenty of free wine.'

'I've just had the Renault overhauled,' Natalie said. 'We thought we might set off in a few days' time. We were planning on doing a week or two's sightseeing before we get there.'

'Be a bit cramped, wouldn't it?' said Ros, 'with four of you in the car.'

'It's summer,' Sarah replied. 'We'd be travelling light. Would you mind?'

'It's all right by me,' Ewart said.

'Great dad!' Sarah flung her arms around his neck. 'We'll bring you a few good bottles back. Thanks, mum!'

Ros also submitted as she was hugged and kissed. And then Sarah and Natalie hurried out in a rush of relief and enthusiasm.

Ros had not bothered to raise any real objections to the holiday, even though she felt she should have. In truth, she found the idea of Sarah going away for a while rather convenient. She and Ewart were heading towards a crisis point, and it was better if Sarah wasn't around to muddy the waters. Even so, she automatically said, 'I'm not sure that was wise, Ewart. None of them are exactly adults.'

'Why didn't you say something, then, if you objected?'

'You'd already given her permission before I had a chance.'

He sighed. 'There's four of them, Ros, and they're all sensible. They're almost adults, and they're not going to do anything silly.'

'I sincerely hope not. But I certainly think we should have a talk with all of them before they leave, just to make sure.'

'Of course.'

It was Ros's turn to sigh. 'Well, at least our daughter has her holiday sorted out, I suppose.'

'We can have one too,' he said placatingly. 'There's still time. Even if we get the go-ahead for the new night-shift, it will probably be at least a month or even more before it actually starts.'

Even now she could sense the anticipation in his voice, as though he could hardly wait. She rose from the table, not saying anything. The food on her plate was cold, whereas Ewart had eaten all his. She picked up both plates and carried them through into the kitchen.

Charlie woke abruptly to the sound of a door slamming. He was slumped in a sofa, with his feet up on the arm of a chair. In front of him, the television was blaring out some routine American TV cop series.

He sat up blearily, assuming that the door had slammed on the screen. It was ten minutes to midnight, and he had fallen asleep over two hours before. Suddenly Liz walked into the room.

'Aarrgghh!' said Charlie, faking a heart attack through fright. Clutching his chest, he fell off the sofa on to the floor.

Liz peered down at him. 'Get up, you fool.'

'I thought it was a burglar. I'd got so used to being on my own here.'

'Very funny.'

She took off her black suede overcoat and draped it over the back of the sofa. Underneath she was dressed in a trendy mid-blue jumpsuit, all zips and baggy limbs.

'I've hardly seen you all this week,' said Charlie, still lying on the floor.

'I can't help it if you keep falling asleep before I get in.'

'It's those early mornings. I've never liked the day shift. So what's been happening on your whirlwind social calendar?'

'Nick and I took Gavin – Mr Brownlow – out for a posh meal.'

'The whizz-kid from London? So it's Gavin now, is it?'

'He's been here over a fortnight, Charlie. It's natural we should all be on first-name terms by now.'

'I should think so – you and Nick have been entertaining him every other night since he arrived.'

'It's important. We might need his backing.'

'So you're buttering him up.'

'If that's what you want to call it – yes. We happen to think it's important. You're not the only person who's committed to his career, you know.'

'Ouch,' said Charlie, sitting up. 'Looks like I touched a nerve.'

'You're so bloody cynical sometimes. And flippant with it.'

He stood up and moved towards her. 'I always get crotchety when I'm sex-starved.'

He was joking, but she broke away from him and stalked into the bathroom, closing the door behind her. Presently he heard the shower running. From the television came the sounds of gunfire and shouting. Charlie could still smell the cigar smoke which had been clinging to Liz's hair.

Headphones on, stockinged feet up on the coffee table, Ewart was listening to Glenn Gould play Mozart. A virtuoso pianist who had first performed in public at the tender age of fourteen, Gould was Ewart's favourite performer, a pianist whose fingers moved over the keyboard with remarkable speed and delicacy.

Caught up in the music, he was totally relaxed. It had been weeks since he had listened to any of his large collection of records, but now the enjoyment was back in profusion once more. Indeed, he felt a renewed appetite for most things in life.

Suddenly, as though by some subliminal trigger, he

knew that Ros had entered the room. Since lunch she had been in a muted state of hostility towards him, speaking only minimally and rejecting any attempts of his to strike up a proper conversation. He knew he had been inconsiderate towards her, but now she seemed to be refusing to allow him to make amends. And so he had sought sanctuary in his record collection, secluded in the music room, while she had remained in the living room, staring grim-faced at the television all evening.

He turned his head and saw that she was standing there in her dressing gown. Lip-reading, he saw her say, 'I'm going to bed.' And then she departed without waiting for him to say anything.

Ewart glanced at his wrist, but he had left his watch in the bathroom. However the red numerals on the stereo's digital display told him that it was 00:15.

The record had ended. Ewart took the headphones off and rose, somewhat stiffly; he had been slumped in the armchair for over three hours. The house was silent around him, and he stood there for a moment, as though waiting for something to happen. Then he heard Ros padding across the landing from bathroom to bedroom.

He switched off the stereo, took the record off the turntable and wiped it carefully before replacing it in its sleeve. Then he filed it in its proper place on the shelves below. Methodically, taking his time, as if delaying the moment when he would actually have to join Ros in bed.

He sighed, and finally forced himself to confront the reality of his situation. He wanted the nightshift job not just because he felt it was vitally important – which he did – or simply because he needed to be involved in hospital work. No, there was more to it than that. Ros had been right when she had suggested that he didn't want to spend twenty-four hours a day with her. That was also important.

It wasn't that he didn't love her. But they had long had their separate careers and been totally committed to them. Yet since Ros had given up teaching, he'd sensed that she had wanted him to make the same sacrifice. But he had grown used to the idea of them having a degree of independence from one another, and for him their marriage had remained fresh because they had never lived in one another's pockets. Absence really did make the heart grow fonder, as far as he was concerned. But Ros, in her anxiety to bring them even closer together, was simply making him feel harassed and suffocated with her determination to make them behave like a retired couple. He didn't like the idea because to him it seemed like an admission that the useful working parts of their lives had ended.

He climbed the stairs, determined to express these feelings to her so that everything would be out in the open. The bedroom was already in darkness when he entered, and Ros was lying on her side, with her back to him.

'Ros,' he whispered. 'I have to talk to you.'

4

Rake in hand, Ewart studied the tangle of grass and weeds in the back garden with a distinct lack of enthusiasm. Ros had left an hour earlier to visit her sister in Swindon, while Sarah had departed for France with her friends the previous afternoon. Alone in the house and feeling at a loose end, Ewart had decided that it was finally time he started work on creating a vegetable patch for himself.

The prospect of this task did not exactly fill him with joy, but he reasoned that it might help mollify Ros, who had been sullen and withdrawn ever since their late-night conversation three days ago. He had hoped that by explaining his feelings, it would help clear the air, whereas in fact it seemed to have had the reverse effect. Ros had taken it all very personally, seeing it as a criticism of her rather than an admission of his own shortcomings.

If he could at least begin work on the back garden, she might see it as proof of his good intentions. But somehow he doubted it, just as he doubted whether he would ever make an adequate gardener. He couldn't even tell one weed from another.

It quickly became clear that the rake was hopelessly inadequate for the task of clearing away the tangle. Ewart rummaged in the garden shed and finally found a sickle under a pile of rotting canvas sacks. Its blade was pitted with rust. He tried an experimental swipe, and managed to behead a cluster of thistles. Inside the house, the telephone rang.

Still grasping the sickle, Ewart went inside and picked up the phone. The caller was Norman Parker.

'Good news,' he said without preamble. 'We've got the go-ahead for a permanent night staff on Casualty.'

'That's great news – and fast work, too. I didn't expect to hear from you for a few weeks at least.'

'Well, as it happens, the time was just ripe. We've got an annex spare here since Maternity was moved last month, and we'll be relocating the department there as soon as possible. Even so, I had to fight tooth-and-nail for it. The fact that you're prepared to administrate it swung the thing in our favour.'

'Thanks, Norman – it means a lot to me.'

'Is it convenient for you to come over today to discuss everything in more detail?'

'Yes,' said Ewart, staring at the sickle blade. 'I'm not doing anything that can't wait until next year.'

Huddled in a shop doorway opposite the radio station, Charlie consulted his watch: it was six o'clock.

He puffed on his cigarette, leant against the window, and waited. Sooner or later, Liz would emerge. And if this Gavin Brownlow was with her, he was going to follow them and see what they got up to.

Traffic hurried by on the main road, carrying commuters home to snug houses and cosy families. Charlie took a deep drag, the tip of his cigarette glowing a fierce red. Keep calm, he told himself. You've got no evidence that anything funny is going on.

He was standing in the doorway of a butcher's shop which had closed for the day just before his arrival. The window was filled with white trays bordered with green parsley. Plastic parsley. Liz's radio station occupied the three floors above a men's outfitters directly opposite.

You're like a bloody spy, Charlie told himself, and he knew he was being unfair to Liz. But he had to find out – he had to be sure that everything was above board.

Liz had been out late for the past four nights in a row, and each time she had a different excuse. She'd gone out with an old girlfriend for a few drinks, had been showing Gavin Brownlow some of the city landmarks, had had to work late with Nick on a consumer affairs programme which they were preparing. Charlie was convinced that she had spent every night with the mysterious Mr Brownlow from London.

His watch showed six-fifteen. He lit another cigarette.

'Got a light, pal?' said a lad in his teens who was passing by.

Charlie gave him a light from the tip of his cigarette while continuing to keep an eye on the doorway beside the outfitters from which Liz would emerge. A cluster of four people appeared even as he was looking, but none was Liz. The teenager shuffled off, his cigarette lit, with a mumbled 'Ta'.

People hurried by on the pavement – ladies with bulging bags of shopping, professional men in smart suits which strained over business-lunch bellies, teenage girls with tinny disco music leaking from the headphones of their Walkmen.

Six-twenty.

Charlie knew he was hot-headed and prone to fits of temper which he often regretted. But this was different. He'd been calm with Liz and had asked her straight out the other evening whether anything was going on with her and this Gavin Brownlow. She'd laughed it off, had insisted that it was just a business courtesy to keep him entertained while he was in Holby. She had always had a way of defusing his anger by refusing to take his objections seriously – he'd always liked that side of her because it prevented him from getting up on too many high horses. But on this occasion his suspicions had not been mollified. The more she made light of the subject, the more he had felt she was hiding something. And so now he was huddled in the doorway, ready to spy on her.

Six-twenty-five.

At that moment he suddenly saw Liz emerge, accompanied by a man in dark-blue overcoat whose face was turned away from him. Charlie had already developed a mental picture of Gavin Brownlow as a smooth, attractive man in his thirties or forties – a smart dresser with a clever line in patter. But the man was shorter than he'd imagined, though he still couldn't see his face.

Liz led him off down the street, and they turned a corner. Swiftly Charlie darted out of the doorway to pursue them. But the traffic lights were green and the traffic was heavy. Charlie shuffled impatiently at the crossing, mentally demanding that the lights switch immediately to red. And they did so.

He darted across the road and hurried towards the corner. Liz and the man had turned down a sidestreet filled with bookshops, antique dealers and restaurants. Charlie was just in time to see the two of them enter *The Green Pagoda*, a Pekingese restaurant much favoured by himself and Liz in the past.

This fact was somehow sufficient to convince Charlie that Liz really was two-timing him. His immediate urge was to charge inside the restaurant, confront Liz and the man – whom he was certain was Brownlow – and have a blazing row. That, at least would make him feel a little better. But he realized that it would also be a bit precipitate.

He lingered outside the restaurant for a good ten minutes, letting his anger cool to simmering-point. It was better to walk in on them after they'd had a chance to settle at their table. Then he might be able to see just how intimate they were together.

Smoking a cigarette, he paced up and down the pavement. A part of him knew he was behaving very foolishly, playing the jealous lover without any proof whatsoever that Liz actually was being unfaithful to him. Their relationship had been founded on the basis that they had very separate careers and did not need to tell one another exactly what they were doing every single hour of the day. And so, in that respect, Liz was not actually being secretive with him. But he had to know exactly what was going on now.

Enough of this vacillating, he told himself, and strode into the restaurant.

The Green Pagoda was a small place, discreetly furnished in bamboo and cork, with paper partitions between the tables on which delicate murals had been painted. Ignoring the staff, Charlie went from cubicle to cubicle, searching for Liz. It was early, and most of the tables were empty. But finally he came upon Liz and the man, tucked away in a corner near the kitchen. He had sat at that table with her himself on several occasions.

She and the man were poring over the menu, and Liz looked up in surprise when she saw him.

'Well,' Charlie said with a menacing smile. 'I was just passing by, and I thought I'd drop in.'

It took a moment for Liz to recover her composure; to his disappointment, she had appeared simply surprised rather than guilty or embarrassed.

'What are you doing here?' she asked.

'As I said, I was just passing by. I saw the two of you come in here, so I thought I'd pop in and say hello.'

Liz glanced at her companion, then back at him. She said, 'This is Gavin Brownlow. Mr Brownlow, this is Charlie Fairhead, my boyfriend.'

Brownlow was a squat man in his late forties, his dark hair plastered greasily across his scalp. Charlie was pleased to note that he had a rather squashed-up face and very hairy eyebrows. Not exactly the Adonis type.

Brownlow had also looked surprised by his sudden appearance at the table, but he now stretched out a hand over the table – a hand whose back was covered with dark hair. 'Pleased to meet you.'

'Pleased to meet *you*,' Charlie responded. 'Liz has been telling me a lot about you.'

Liz flashed him a warning look, as if to say 'Don't you dare get bolshie'. But Charlie wasn't going to pull any of his punches.

'Well,' he said, 'this is very cosy.'

'I was treating Gavin to a last meal,' Liz said hastily, 'on the station, before he goes back to London tomorrow.'

Charlie nodded knowingly. To Brownlow he said, 'Had a nice visit, have you?'

'It's been most instructive.'

'Liz has certainly been looking after you while you've been here. I've hardly seen her in the last week or so.'

'She's been an excellent host,' Brownlow agreed.

He looks like a wrestler, Charlie thought, but he talks like a toff. And there was something genuinely innocent in his manner which made Charlie think that perhaps there really was nothing suspicious going on. But he couldn't back down now; he had to be sure. At that moment he noticed an unlit cigar in Brownlow's left hand, and this was sufficient to renew all his suspicions.

'Where's Nick tonight?' he asked Liz.

'He's working late,' she said in a tight, controlled voice.

'So there's just the two of you. Very cosy.'

'Charlie, have you been drinking . . .?'

'Sober as a judge, my darling. As a judge. Isn't this going a bit beyond the bounds of duty?'

'What exactly, Charlie?'

He indicated the whole table. 'This. A quiet nook, tucked away from the world. We used to come here, remember? Very intimate.'

Liz looked rigid with anger, but only now did Brownlow seem to grasp what Charlie was getting at. He frowned, looked at Liz, then back at Charlie. 'What exactly are you implying?'

'I would have thought that it was pretty obvious,' Charlie said.

'It's becoming so. But then I'm never quite sure of things when I'm dealing with innuendo. Perhaps you'd mind spelling it out for me in plain English.'

All of a sudden, Brownlow was quite composed, in control of matters. And his directness took the wind right out of Charlie's argumentative sails.

'It's all right, Gavin . . .' Liz began.

'No,' he said, keeping his eyes on Charlie, 'I'm afraid it's not all right, Liz. Are you implying that there's something going on between Liz and myself?'

'That's what it looks like,' Charlie said wanly.

'Listen, young man,' Brownlow said, making Charlie feel about ten years old, 'I am a married man with three grown-up children. I'm entirely devoted to my family, and I *never* mix business with pleasure.'

A young Chinese waiter had materialized out of the dimness, and he was standing there, holding two platefuls of dark green seaweed, looking bemused. Charlie could

see that Liz was consumed with both anger and mortific-
ation, while Brownlow looked merely annoyed, as if a
persistent fly had been buzzing around his head. At last
Charlie knew for sure that he had made a terrible blunder;
there was nothing going on, and he had made a fool of
himself in order to prove it.

'Oh balls,' he said. And then he walked out.

Back at the flat a half an hour later, Charlie cracked the
first of a six-pack of Carlsberg Special Brew. He intended
to get thoroughly plastered; perhaps then he might be
able to face Liz when she returned home. If she *did*
return.

The telephone rang.

'Charlie Fairhead,' he said morosely into the
mouthpiece.

'Charlie, this is Ewart Plimmer. Have you been at
work? I've been trying to reach you all evening.'

'No, I've been busy making a fool of myself.'

'What?'

'Nothing. What's up?'

'I saw Norman Parker this afternoon. We've got the
go-ahead for the regular night staff and a Casualty
Department that's open permanently. The Director of
Nursing is going to offer you the job of Charge Nurse.'

Immediately Charlie's spirits began to lift.

'Terrific,' he said. 'That's pretty fast work.'

'They'll be moving us into the old Maternity annex at
the hospital. I'll be the Clinical Assistant. Norman Parker
wants it all set up in the next fortnight.'

'Furiouser and furiouser,' said Charlie..

'We've got a year in which to prove ourselves. Parker's
done what he can, but he's under pressure from the

Government to make economies, so we're going to have to make the best of what we're given.'

'That suits me. We can show them we're really needed.'

'You said something to me when we last talked about having a few names in mind for the staff.'

'That's right – I've got a shortlist. They're all good people who would actually enjoy working nights. I think I shall be able to persuade the Director of Nursing that they're the people we need.'

'Good. I think it is time we got together to discuss the set up. Are you available tomorrow?'

'I'm on days. Tell you what – I'll meet you in Max's Café at half past three.'

'Max's Café?'

'It's just down the road from the hospital – bit of a glorified transport café, really, but its always been popular with nursing staff and ambulance crews. Don't find many consultant surgeons in there, though.'

'That's fine by me. It sounds like the sort of place I'll be needing to get to know.'

'You bet you will – especially on the night shift. It's the only place for miles that's open twenty-four hours a day.'

'OK, I'll see you there at three-thirty.'

'Look forward to it.'

Ewart rang off. Charlie put the receiver down, and a smile of triumph creased his face. For six months or more he had nurtured the hope that a regular night-shift could be set up in Casualty, but he had never expected to snare Ewart Plimmer into running it. Ewart's acceptance had confirmed in spades Charlie's high opinion of him.

He drank down half of his lager and lit a cigarette. The door opened, and in walked Liz.

'Drowning your sorrows?' she said, her face still like thunder.

73

'Liz, I'm sorry. I really am.'

She tossed her shoulder-bag on to the armchair opposite him. 'So you damn well should be. Just what was the big idea?'

'I thought you were fooling around with him.'

'Fooling around with him? He's not exactly my type.'

Charlie simply shrugged.

'What did you do? Follow us?'

He nodded.

'You ought to be ashamed of yourself.'

'Don't worry, I am. Made a right prat of myself in that restaurant. And I know it must have been even worse for you.'

'Too bloody true. Especially since he'd just offered me a job.'

'A job?'

Liz had taken off her coat, and now she slumped in the armchair.

'In London. With City Sound.'

Charlie simply stared at her. City Sound was one of the major commercial radio stations in the capital, and for Liz it would represent a huge career advancement.

'Twelve till four slot, five days a week. On three times the salary I'm earning now.'

'And I cocked it up for you?'

'Not exactly. But you can certainly pick your moment.'

'So he offered you the job?'

She nodded. 'That's why Nick wasn't there – he doesn't know anything about it. And that's why I've been out with him every other evening – *he's* been wining and dining *me*, trying to lure me away to City Sound. Apparently he really likes the way I operate – but strictly professionally.'

'And so he should. You're damned good at your job. So what did you say?'

'I told him I'd think about it.'

'I'd have thought you'd have jumped at the chance.'

'I wanted to talk to you about it first. If I took the job, and if the two of us are to stay together, then it would mean you moving back to London with me.'

Charlie hadn't considered this. 'You couldn't commute?'

'No chance. This would be a high-pressure job, Charlie. They'd want me there ten hours a day. Phone-ins, interviews, outside broadcasts – the lot.'

'Are you keen?'

'Of course I'm keen. You know I've been chafing at the bit, hoping for a big break.'

'But I thought you wanted to stay in Holby.'

'Well, I'm not *that* mad on London. But then again it's an opportunity that's too good to miss. And if we both went, things would be a lot easier.'

Charlie could tell that she had been thinking long and hard about it, weighing up the pros and cons.

'There's a problem, Liz. I've just heard that we've got the go-ahead for a new regular night-shift on Casualty. With me as Charge Nurse.'

She reached across and took a cigarette from his packet, lighting it up. She smoked only rarely, in moments of stress or indecision.

'I see,' she said, exhaling smoke. 'And you want the job, don't you?'

He nodded. 'I've been fighting for it for months. It's important to me. As important as this job is to you.'

'So what are you saying?'

'I'm not sure. I don't want to stand in the way of your

career, Liz, and I also want us to stay together. But I'm already committed to this new job.'

Ash fell from Liz's cigarette on to her skirt. She brushed it away. 'It seems like we've got a few incompatibilities there.'

'I got the phonecall about the job just before you walked in.'

'So what if you'd got it after I'd told you about my offer? What would you have said then?'

Charlie did not reply, but he knew that Liz could tell he would still have accepted it.

'Well, lover boy,' she said, crushing out her cigarette in the ashtray, 'looks like I've got some serious thinking to do.'

She rose. Charlie took her arm.

'Liz, I mean it – I don't want us to split up.'

She smiled down at him, but there was something distant in it.

'Maybe not, Charlie. But the question is – just what sort of sacrifices are you prepared to make to stop it happening?'

Ewart had spent most of the evening listening to Glenn Gould play Beethoven's piano concertos, and he was now fully replete in a musical sense. Gould's career had always fascinated him, not least because he was the same age as Ewart and displayed the kind of musical gifts which Ewart would have loved to possess himself. Way back in 1957, Ewart had made a pilgrimage to Berlin to see Gould's European debut with Karajan. Since the mid '60s, Gould had made very few concert appearances, preferring to record, and this made Ewart's memory of his live performance one to be treasured more than most.

He had rung Ros's sister's house several times that

evening, but there had been no reply. No doubt the two women were out visiting other relatives who lived round about. Ros had told him that she would probably be late home, but Ewart now saw that it was approaching midnight. He began to entertain a grim vision of Ros's car smashed to bits on the M4 and of her broken body being loaded into the back of an ambulance. He was heading towards the phone when it started ringing.

'Ewart Plimmer,' he said into the mouthpiece.

'It's me,' said Ros's voice.

'Where are you? Are you all right?'

'I'm at Madge's still. She invited me to stay over the night, and I've decided to.'

'Oh. Fine.'

There was a silence.

'Are you sure you're OK?' Ewart asked. 'You sound a bit – remote.'

'I'm fine. I'll call you tomorrow, before I set off.'

'Hang on a minute. I've got some news.'

Silence.

'Ros? Are you there?'

'I'm here.'

'I've heard from the hospital. About the night-shift. They want it all set up in a couple of weeks.'

There was a pause before she said, 'You must be very pleased.'

'That doesn't mean we can't have a holiday.'

'No?'

'If we organize it now, then I can tell them exactly when I want to have my leave.'

'I'll call you tomorrow.'

'Wait a minute,' he began, but did not know what to say afterwards. 'How's Madge?'

'Not too good, actually. Her arthritis has been playing her up.'

Madge was a widow, ten years older than Ros.

'Send her my love,' Ewart said.

'I always do. Whether you ask me to or not.'

Ewart was by now thoroughly unnerved by the tenor of the conversation. Ros was curt to the point of unfriendliness.

'You might have let me know earlier that you were staying over,' he said. 'I was worried about you.'

'Oh? Why didn't you call earlier yourself then?'

'I did.'

'We've both been here since seven. The phone hasn't rung.'

'I called at five. And at six. There was no reply.'

'We were out.'

Again there was a silence.

'It's late,' Ros said. 'I'll call you tomorrow.'

The line went dead.

5

Max's Café was a long, low building of pebble-dashed walls and white-painted windows draped with net curtains. It stood on the corner of two busy roads a hundred yards from the City Hospital, with ample parking space in its wide forecourt for lorries, ambulances and cars. Architecturally undistinguished and with a decor that tended to the basic, it was popular because it served plain but wholesome food at very reasonable prices, plus half-pint mugs of tea and coffee at 15p a time. It was most famed for its cakes and buns, delivered fresh from the bakery just down the road twice a day.

Charlie was tired after his shift, and so he had driven the short distance between the hospital and the café. He parked next to a big container truck which was carrying frozen fish.

It was a quiet time of the day, and there were no other vehicles in the car park. A sign above the door announced the café's name in red lettering on a green background. It looked like a colour-blindness test.

Inside Max, a squat, balding Australian, was ensconced behind the counter, his white apron spotless. He was in his fifties, and had come to England after the war, marrying a local girl named Mavis. Together they had run the café ever since, Mavis doing the cooking and he serving the customers.

'Tea,' Max said as Charlie approached the counter. 'Milk and two sugars.'

'You've got it,' Charlie said. Max knew all the regulars

from the hospital well, and he always seemed to be on duty, no matter what the time of day or night.

'Don't you ever sleep?' Charlie asked him.

'Not if I can help it,' Max said, pouring Charlie's tea from a gleaming chrome-plated urn. He put the cup down on the counter. 'Anything else?'

Charlie studied the blackboard on the wall behind Max which gave details of the day's menu.

'*Hack* and chips,' said Charlie, reading the words scrawled in chalk. '*Stake* and kidney pie?'

Max looked around. He studied the board as if noticing the words for the first time.

'That's the temporary chef,' he said with disgust. 'Can't bloody spell to save his life. Can't bloody cook too great, either, if you ask me.'

'So where's Mavis?'

'A guest at your hotel down the road. She's finally gone in to have her gallstone taken out.'

Charlie remembered that Mavis had been waiting for the operation for six months or more.

'Mr Croome's operating,' Max said. 'He any good?'

'One of the best,' Charlie told him. 'She'll be in good hands.'

'That's something, anyway.' Max looked morose for a moment. Then suddenly he yelled: 'Morton!!'

A few moments later a man wearing a crumpled chef's hat appeared from the kitchen. He was tall and lean and looked to be in his mid-twenties. His apron was splattered with egg-yoke, gravy and pinkish stains which looked to Charlie like blood from raw meat. There was a rather gormless expression on his face and a dew-drop hung from the end of his red nose. He held a plate on which was a yellowish-grey mass.

Max pointed at the blackboard. 'That's *not* the way to spell hake, Morton. Or steak.'

'Uh,' said Morton, 'does it matter? As long as everyone knows what it is.'

'It matters to me,' said Max. 'Didn't you ever learn to spell properly?'

'I'm a cook,' said Morton through his nose, as though that were explanation enough. He sniffed heavily through liquid nostrils.

'You could have fooled me,' Max replied, peering at the plate. 'What's that?'

'Scrambled egg on toast. For the bloke over there.'

Morton indicated the only other customer, a lorry driver in a donkey jacket who was sitting at a table, nursing a mug of tea.

'In future,' said Max, 'you write out the menu on a piece of paper, and I'll put it up on the blackboard.'

'Ah,' said Morton, 'ah – ah – ah – '

Frantically he put the plate down on the counter. Then he sneezed heavily, causing Max to leap back to avoid being sprayed. Charlie watched with a kind of ghastly fascination as he produced an incredibly grubby handkerchief and proceeded to blow his nose. Then he put the handkerchief back in the pocket of his apron, picked up the plate of scrambled eggs, and carried it off to the driver.

'Useless,' Max said, staring after him. 'He's a bloody menace about the place.'

'How did you find him?' Charlie asked.

'Recommended to me by a friend – who just happened to be his uncle. I'd pay him off, except that I haven't got the time to find anyone else with Mavis being in hospital. You know something – every day I've got to remind him

81

to wash his hands before he starts work. There's more sense in a strawberry.'

Max was still watching Morton as he shuffled off back to the kitchen. Charlie could see the driver inspecting his scrambled egg like a bacteriologist poring over a culture on a slide. Giving his full attention to Charlie, Max said, 'So what'll it be? We've got the usual – chips with everything – and the special's lasagne.'

'Forget it,' said Charlie. 'I'll just have a doughnut.'

Max used a pair of tongs to retrieve the doughnut from the glass display cabinet beside the counter; he, at least, always paid great attention to hygiene. The café held three rows of yellow-topped melamine tables, with chairs of plyboard and tubular steel. The mustard-coloured walls were hung with old postcards, calendars, beermats, soccer badges – anything which the customers wanted to donate to brighten up the place. It was hardly the Ritz, but Max kept it scrupulously clean and the atmosphere was always good-natured.

Charlie carried his tea and doughnut over to a table beside the window. Two ambulance men entered, nodding at Charlie as they ordered a three-course meal. Charlie knew them both well, and he was tempted to shout at them to stick to cakes. But he didn't want to hurt Max's feelings.

He lit a cigarette and sipped his tea, staring out through the net curtain at the car park. It was three-twenty, and Ewart Plimmer would be arriving soon; he was always punctual. Charlie took a piece of paper from his jacket pocket, unfolded it and studied the list which he had composed. It ran all the way down the page, but many of the names had been crossed out, and only three were ringed. These were the ones whom Charlie was most keen to have as his staff on the shift.

A young woman entered the café and approached the counter. For a moment, Charlie thought it was Liz, but then he saw that it was a stranger. Last night he and Liz had gone to bed and made love without having any further discussion over what they were going to do about their respective futures. Their lovemaking had had a fierceness which was almost desperate, as though they were having a final frantic fling before everything ended. Charlie had never considered himself an indecisive type, but for once he really didn't know what to do for the best. Liz might resent him if she turned down the job because he didn't want to move back to London; and he would resent her if he was forced to go with her just when his ambitions for the department had been realized. He couldn't do it. Couldn't.

He ate his doughnut and lit another cigarette. A few students from the local polytechnic were now trickling into the café. Someone at the counter was asking for black pudding and baked beans with curried eggs. And in the kitchen, Morton was having another sneezing fit.

Traffic was heavy in the city centre, and Ewart was late. He drummed his fingers on the driving wheel as he waited at the red light. The dashboard clock showed three-thirty-five.

He turned to his passenger. 'Listen, Joyce, would you mind if I dropped you off here?'

'Here?' said Joyce. 'In the middle of the road?'

'It's safe while the light's on red. Woolworth's is just around the corner.'

'It's changed,' Joyce said, just as the driver behind him began parping his horn.

Ewart put the car into gear and drove off, further resentment growing in him. Joyce had 'just popped in for a chat' a half an hour before he was due to set off for his meeting with Charlie Fairhead, and she had pretended surprise at not finding Ros there. In fact, Ros had rung him earlier from Madge's to say that she had decided to stay at her sister's for a few more days. Madge wasn't too well, she claimed, and she was going to look after her for a short while. Ewart himself had few illusions that this was a mild and socially acceptable form of ostracism – a punishment for what Ros saw as his selfishness. What bothered him most was that he had actually been relieved to hear that she wasn't coming home immediately.

He had told Joyce none of this, of course, merely explaining that Ros was looking after her sister in Swindon. He was pretty sure she knew exactly when Ros had gone away, for she was the archetypal nosy neighbour, constantly peering out from behind her net curtains to monitor the comings and goings of others on the estate. Sometimes Ewart felt sorry for her because she was obviously lonely: her husband was a businessman who spent weeks and sometimes months abroad, and they had no children. But at other times she simply annoyed him with her inquisitiveness, her intrusions on other people's lives.

As she did now. When he had mentioned that he was driving into town, she had requested a lift so that she could buy some rose bushes from Woolworth's – she didn't drive herself. He had been happy to oblige, but he had not anticipated that it would take her twenty minutes to get ready. And so now he was running late, and she was still insisting that he drop her right outside the store.

He turned the corner and almost ran into a parked car. Calm down, he told himself; concentrate on the road.

'I thought this was a one-way street,' said Joyce.

'No,' Ewart replied, frantically checking his rear-view

mirror to ensure that other cars were following him since there were none ahead. For a horrible second he thought that he might have suffered a brainstorm and had totally forgotten the city's road system. But cars *were* following him; he was all right.

He pulled up outside Woolworth's, leaving the engine running.

'Thank you, Ewart,' Joyce said, making no attempt to get out.

'You're welcome,' he said.

'If there's anything I can do for you while Ros is away – you only have to let me know.'

Just go! he thought vehemently. But he forced a smile and said, 'I will.'

'Anything I can get you from the shops?'

'No, no. I really must be going.'

She nodded, then started fumbling with the door handle. The door refused to open.

'I can never get the hang of these things,' she told him.

'You need to unlock it.'

'How?'

'The black button at the bottom of the window.'

'Where?'

I don't believe this! Ewart thought. He reached across and unlocked the door, having to lean across her. She was wearing violet-scented perfume – rather too much of it.

'Thank you,' she said.

'Don't forget your seat-belt.'

She unstrapped herself, shrugged out of it. She was several years younger than Ros, and a reasonably fit woman. Even so it seemed to take her ages to actually climb out of the car. As if she's doing it deliberately, Ewart thought.

85

''Bye,' he said, pulling the door shut behind her.

She began to reach forward as if to knock on the window pane. Pretending he hadn't noticed, Ewart drove off at speed.

A few minutes later, he turned into the car park of Max's Café. The garish sign in red and green was a beacon visible for hundreds of yards away, and he had had no difficulty in finding the place.

Inside it was crowded, filled with steam and the smell of fried food. He spotted Charlie sitting alone at a table by the window.

'I thought you weren't coming,' Charlie said as he sat down.

'Had to make a detour to drop a neighbour off,' Ewart told him. 'I was beginning to think I'd never get here.'

Charlie fetched him a tea, and then they settled down to business. Ewart filled him in with the details of his meeting with Norman Parker, and then Charlie produced a list.

Ewart studied the names on the paper. 'Most of these have been crossed out.'

'I put down as many names as I could think of to start with. Then I whittled them down a bit.'

'What about these three?' Ewart asked, indicating the ringed names:

CLIVE KING

MEGAN ROACH

D. DUFFIN

'I could have come up with more,' Charlie told him, 'but they're the hard core, the ones I know well. They each have good reasons for wanting to work nights, and I think they'll give me their all. I can also vouch for them being good at their jobs.'

Ewart swallowed a mouthful of tea. 'Tell me something about them?'

'Clive King's a staff nurse, about forty years old. He was born in Jamaica, but his parents moved to England when he was small, and he's lived in Holby ever since. A big bloke in all senses of the word, and a solid, dependable type.'

Ewart nodded. The mention of Jamaica set Ewart thinking about the holiday he and Ros were supposed to be having. Something told him it would never materialize.

'Megan Roach's an SEN. She's in her fifties, and she's had more experience of hospital work than I've had hot dinners. Knows the work inside out, and she's good at calming things down if they get too hectic or getting things moving if they're a bit slack. Handles people really well.'

'That could be useful with some of the stranger types we're likely to get coming in at night.'

'That's what I thought. She'd be a stabilizing influence for the younger staff.'

'And D. Duffin – what does the D. stand for?'

'Search me – I think it must be a state secret. Everyone knows her as Duffy. She's a local girl, just finished her training. She's still got a lot to learn, but she's eager and dedicated – and a bit of a character. Got slightly mystical tendencies, if you ask me, but she's very down-to-earth in her work. We're going to need some young blood, and she's the best type.'

'Well, that's three pretty good character references. What about the other names on the list?'

'All recommended, but those are the three I'd give priority to.'

'Fair enough. Would you mind if I went to see them?

Your staff, I know, but I thought the personal touch might help a bit.'

Charlie gave a knowing smile, then produced another piece of paper. 'I guessed that might be your style. That's why I made a list of their addresses as well.'

Ewart took it from him.

'Any idea what doctor's going to be attached to the shift?' Charlie asked.

'Lawrence Clarke,' Ewart said. 'He'll be on a six month contract. Do you know him?'

'I know him,' Charlie replied. 'And I can't say I'm impressed. He's a bit of a know-all, without the experience to back it up.'

Ewart smiled, knowing that Charlie tended to take strong likes or dislikes towards people. 'I think I should keep an open mind until I've interviewed him. Now I'm going to feed my face a bit – didn't manage lunch today. What's the food like in this place?'

'Normally, it's pretty good. Basic but appetizing. Trouble is, Mavis isn't cooking it at the moment.'

'She's the chef?'

'The cook – "chef" would be far too grand for her.'

'So what would you recommend?'

'With Morton doing the cooking, I'd advise that you stick to a lettuce leaf or a digestive biscuit.'

Suddenly the whole café was filled with the loud sound of someone blowing his nose. The noise was explosive enough to silence the patrons, and Ewart stared at Charlie with a questioning look.

'That,' said Charlie, 'was Morton.'

6

The luminous hands on the bedside clock told Clive King that it was five minutes to six. Beside him his wife, Leah, was sleeping peacefully, soft snores issuing from her mouth. Clive stared up at the ceiling, feeling tense, deserted by sleep. A growing rumble in the distance told him that a train was approaching – the five o'clock from Cardiff, he guessed.

Around him the house was still and silent, but he had not slept in the last hour. For the past few days he had been working the afternoon shift, and he was due in again today at three o'clock. He needed more sleep before then. But he knew that there was little chance of that.

He sat up, leaning back against the padded headboard of the bed. Through the crack in the curtains he could see that a pale dawn was seeping into the sky over the clutter of rooftops and chimneys. The sound of the train was louder now, but he could tell that it was slowing down as it pulled into Holby Central Station.

It wasn't the noise of the trains that kept him awake during the night, for he slept well enough by day, when they were more frequent and you could even hear the announcements over the tannoy. The station was less than a hundred yards away from the house, but all the family were accustomed to its traffic. He didn't really know why he was only able to snatch an hour or two between midnight and dawn; when he was on nights, he slept a good eight hours immediately after the shift.

His GP had prescribed Mogadons for the problem, but he didn't like taking them – in the mornings he felt as if he had been hit on the head with a brick. So he'd sought advice from his colleagues at the hospital, and one of the Sisters had confessed to a similar problem, which she had learned to deal with. Make a virtue out of a vice, she'd told him; if you can't sleep, then don't just lie there worrying about it – get up and do something. Read a book, or do a crossword, or make model aeroplanes. The trouble was, he invariably felt too tired to do these things, even though he couldn't sleep.

From the bedroom next door came a snorting sound, then a sleepy murmur. Clive stiffened, waiting for further sounds. But all was silent. He did not move for five minutes, until he was sure that his father had subsided back into a deep sleep.

Leah rolled over, her hand resting lightly on his hip. He lifted it gently and slipped out of bed, putting on his dressing gown and slippers. He was a tall man of six foot three, and powerfully built. Football had always been the passion which had kept him fit – a passion which he had also passed on to his two young sons.

Opening the bedroom door very carefully so not to make any noise, he crept across the landing, past his father's door, and entered the bathroom. He drank a glass of water, studied his face in the toothpaste-spotted mirror above the sink. His Mogadons were in the cabinet next to the mirror.

He removed the bottle, unscrewed the cap, paused. Then he tipped the entire contents down the toilet and flushed it.

After the noise of running water had subsided, he listened for any sounds from the bedrooms. There were none. Cautiously he opened the door. I'm like a burglar in my own house, he told himself, and grinned spontaneously.

Edging open the door of the boys' bedroom, he peered inside. Errol and Bobby were lying together, looking as if they had fallen asleep in the middle of a wrestling match. Around them was a clutter of toys – *Star Wars* spaceships and figures, bits of Lego, Spiderman and Batman masks, and various comics.

Smiling, Clive gently drew the bedclothes over their sleeping bodies. Errol was nine, Bobby seven, and both boys were a delight to him. Above their bed was stretched the red and white scarf of Holby United, and below it a team photograph of the First Division side. They had barely escaped relegation last season, and had lost their opening home game the previous Saturday, much to the boys' disappointment. He had promised to take them to as many home games as possible, and he was hoping that the side's fortunes would improve. Standing on wet terraces every other Saturday, watching your team getting played off the park was a dismal experience.

Clive exited, pulling the door gently shut behind him. He crept back along the landing, then paused outside his father's bedroom. The bolt was firmly drawn on the outside of the door. He put his ear against the panel and listened. He was able to make out his father's heavy, asthmatic breathing – he was sound asleep. Clive felt himself relaxing; nights were often the most difficult times with the old man, but recently he had been taking his sedatives without protest and so had been sleeping more peacefully.

He entered his own bedroom, and Leah immediately said, 'What are you doing up?'

'Couldn't sleep,' he told her. Sufficient light was now filtering through the crack in the curtains for him to see

her face. She was a handsome woman, born in Jamaica
and raised in Holby just like him. In school, they had
been childhood sweethearts – it seemed corny now, but
he recalled the memories fondly. Like him she was tall
and strongly built, though oddly both their boys were of
average size, neither large nor small. Leah confidently
predicted that they would both put on a spurt of growth
before they went to secondary school; he himself had
actually been small in stature until he'd reached the age
of ten.

'Dad's asleep,' he said. 'The kids, too.'

'Come to bed, then.'

'I can't get off to sleep.'

She grinned at him in the twilight. 'There's other things
to do.'

Clive was having breakfast with the boys when the minister called in. Errol and Bobby were arguing over who
was to have possession of the green plastic goblin at the
bottom of the cereal packet, and he was adjudicating.

'*I'm* having it,' he told them, since it seemed the
simplest option.

They both began to protest, but he was adamant.
'Finish up your toast and tea. I don't want to hear another
word out of you.'

'But dad – ' both boys chorused.

'Not another word.'

At this point Leah entered with Raymond Hurley, the
white-haired and bespectacled minister of St Andrews
Baptist Church. Clive was a deacon there, and both he
and Leah had been committed Baptists since their teens.
The St Andrews area of Holby held a mixed population
of roughly equal proportions of blacks and whites. Ray
Hurley and his wife had adopted a young black girl

several years ago to add to their own family of four boys. He was widely respected in the area by all sections of the community.

'Morning, Clive,' he said, smiling. 'And how are these two budding soccer stars this morning?'

'We've got practice in an hour,' Errol said instantly.

'On the Church Field,' added Bobby.

'When's the next game?' Ray Hurley asked.

'This Saturday,' said Errol. 'The semi-finals of the Samuels Cup.'

'We're playing Riverside Rovers,' Bobby told him. 'Their defence is a bit suspect.'

'*You'll* be a bit suspect,' Clive said firmly, 'if you don't eat up your breakfast. I want to see both those plates clear, otherwise there'll be no football practice at all.'

The two boys immediately began to show a great interest in their toast.

'I came to see your father,' Ray Hurley told Clive.

Clive nodded; he had suspected as much. Leah said, 'My mother's with him upstairs.'

Clive rose from the table, intending to accompany them.

'Dad,' said Errol, 'if I score a goal this morning, can I have the goblin?'

'That's not fair,' Bobby protested. 'You're a striker and I'm a centre-back.'

'We'll settle this right now,' Clive said. He delved into his trouser pocket and produced the green goblin. Before the startled eyes of the boys he popped it into his mouth. And swallowed.

'There,' he said. 'That's ended that.'

The two boys were stunned into silence. Clive followed Leah and the minister into the hallway, closing the door behind him.

93

'You didn't, did you?' Leah asked.

Clive grinned and shook his head. He poked out his tongue. The goblin was sitting on it. He raised a hand and took it off, slipping it back into his pocket.

'I hid it under my tongue,' he told Leah and the minister as they climbed the stairs.

'Sometimes,' Leah remarked, 'I reckon you're as big a kid as they are. And you still haven't solved the problem – who's going to get it?'

'We had the same problem with the last cereal packet,' Clive told her. 'I kept that prize, too.' From his other pocket he produced another plastic object, this one a red dragon. 'After the football practice I'll tell them I've still got both of them. There'll be one in each closed fist. They can choose which hand they want – left or right. Then they'll have to take whatever they get.'

Ray Hurley beamed. 'The wisdom of Solomon.'

'That's the theory, anyway,' Clive said. 'In practice, they'll probably still squabble whatever they get.'

The lightness of mood quickly evaporated as they reached the top of the stairs. Now Clive could feel himself growing tense once more.

They crossed the landing, and Leah opened the door to the bedroom. Her mother, Lucy, was sitting at the bedside, holding a spoon and a dish of mushy Weetabix and milk. His father was sitting up in bed, a white napkin stuffed under his ample chin.

Like his son, Colin King was a big man, though largeness had become fatness in his old age. His grey-white hair had not been cut in months – the old man would not allow it – and now it formed a dense cloud around his head. His eyes were as bright as ever, but there was a strange intensity in them combined with an equally strange lack of focus. When he stared at his son,

Clive had the feeling that his father was looking straight through him.

Ray Hurley moved forward to the bedside, smiling. 'Morning, Colin. How are you this morning?'

Colin King glared at him suspiciously, then glanced at Lucy.

'It's Mr Hurley,' she told him. 'From the church. You remember.'

The old man's expresion did not alter, but his right hand began snatching spasmodically at the bedclothes. Bits of Weetabix bordered his mouth, though he had evidently eaten little of what was in the bowl. Clive hung back, as if seeking shelter behind Leah and the minister.

'They're trying to poison me,' he said. 'Especially him.'

The old man's finger was bent with arthritis, but it pointed unambiguously at Clive.

'Of course he's not,' Leah said, gently but firmly. 'Why would he want to do a thing like that?'

'When he was little, he used to put flies in my soup. Now it's drugs.'

Clive had a vague memory of dropping a dead fly in his father's gumbo once while they had still been living in Kingston. He had done it as a joke, and at the time his father had laughed. But it was no laughing matter now.

'The drugs aren't meant to harm you,' the minister told the old man. 'They'll make you feel better.'

Colin King snatched more fiercely at the bedclothes. 'Keep him away from me.'

Clive stared at his father's face – a face haunted with suspicion and confusion.

'I'll go downstairs,' he said in a small voice. Leah gave him a smile of sympathy and sorrow as he retreated, closing the door behind him.

Downstairs the kids were gone, the breakfast table

littered with the debris of their toast. Clive went to the kitchen window and saw them out in the back garden, riding their bikes up and down the paths, laughing and tugging at one another. As he stared at them, he thought of his father in his prime – a strapping man with a gentle nature and a ready smile. He had worked in Holby Docks after they'd come to England, supporting the family by labouring fourteen hours a day unloading cargo vessels of everything from sacks of grain to crates of tea. Now he was scarcely recognizable as the same man – especially in his manner.

Clive ran a hand over his lips. He was trembling. It had all begun with the death of his mother. She'd suffered a heart attack eight years previously, though she had been ill for some time before that so that none of the family had been entirely unprepared. But his father, who had always loved her dearly, had immediately lapsed into a moody and withdrawn state. At first the family had assumed that he was simply suffering from deep grief, but as weeks had turned into months and his father's mood had grown more wayward, Clive had begun to realize that something more was wrong. His father wasn't eating, he had begun to ramble, talking a lot about the old days in Jamaica while at the same time becoming increasingly confused about present-day things such as remembering to wash and clean himself after visiting the toilet.

Eventually Clive had got the doctor to visit – the old man had refused point-blank to visit the surgery – and the GP had confirmed what Clive had suspected, and dreaded, most. Alzheimer's Disease, a progressive form of senile dementia for which there was no cure.

Clive knew all about the syndrome, how it was called the Silent Epidemic since if affected perhaps as many as one in ten elderly people in the country as a whole. But his medical knowledge of the exact nature of the disease did not equip him to deal with it emotionally, especially since his father's increasing paranoia and hostility – common symptoms of the ailment – were directed most at him. Nothing he could do would please the old man; everything his father found fault with was in some way his fault.

Clive watched the boys in the garden, and their youthful vigour only sharpened the despair and melancholy which he felt. His father's illness had been a severe test to his faith, and the trial continued. Sometimes he thought sacrilegious thoughts, wondering how a merciful God could allow one of his creations to decline into death with so little dignity and such a lack of awareness of his plight; sometimes he would want to scream with the injustice of it all. At nights his father would sometimes go wandering, and once they had found him out on the main road, in danger of being knocked down and with no knowledge of where he was. So they had been forced to put a lock on his bedroom door to protect him from himself. But that did not make Clive feel any less like a jailer, especially since his father frequently accused him of being just that.

Friends had advised them to have the old man put in a home where he could be properly looked after, but both he and Leah had decided against that. Leah's mother, a widow, dropped by every day to help her look after the old man, and he tolerated her better than most, allowing her to feed him. At times he was just like a huge baby, and the sight of him made Clive want to weep.

But his faith – and the support of the rest of his family – had also been a source of comfort to him. Whenever he felt near the end of his tether, he would go to the church and pray, or visit Mr Hurley at his home. The minister had counselled him well, reminding him that God moves in mysterious ways, and that his father's sickness might be a test of his, Clive's, faith. He should not waver, but remain steadfast in his belief.

Well, he had remained steadfast. But sometimes he needed a little extra help. Like now.

He went through into the living room and took a small key out of a white china vase on the drinks cabinet. Opening its door, he removed a bottle of Haig whisky and a glass tumbler. He filled the tumbler halfway and swallowed a mouthful before putting the bottle back and locking the door. He dropped the key in the vase and returned to the kitchen.

Now the boys were digging holes in the tiny lawn with a plastic spade left over from their summer holidays. Clive took another mouthful of his scotch, deciding against shouting out to them to stop.

The liquor settled through his body like a warm river, and immediately he could feel his tensions beginning to diminish. Then he heard Leah and Mr Hurley's voices on the landing. After a moment, their footsteps began to descend the stairs. He swallowed the rest of his drink in one, then swiftly rinsed the glass in the sink.

A cloudburst had forced the abrupt abandonment of the football practice after only ten minutes. Clive and the eleven boys in his charge were huddled in the old pavilion beside the Church Field, watching the rain pour down from a slate-grey sky.

'Think it'll stop soon, dad?' asked Bobby.

'Maybe,' said Clive. 'We'll give it ten more minutes.'

'The roof's leaking,' Errol said, pointing upwards. Water was dripping down on to the wooden floor from a gap in the slates.

The pavilion was semi-derelict, but it was an adequate shelter on a warm summer day. Nearby stood the church after which the fields – there were actually several – had been named. It was a Victorian building, with a red brick tower and plenty of crenellations, but it had been built on the bones of a structure that dated back to the 13th century. Compared to Jamaica, England had always seemed an incredibly old country to Clive.

Though the practice had been cut short, Clive was confident that his team were in good fettle for the semi-final on Saturday. The St Andrews Strollers, as they were called, belonged to the Holby Youth League, and Clive had been training them for the past two seasons. Since he had taken over, they'd risen from a lowly position in the league and were now challenging for third place. And if they won the Samuels Cup – a new competition sponsored by a wealthy local businessman who had a keen eye for publicity – it would be the first trophy the team had ever won.

The rain began to slacken to a drizzle, and the boys started to plead for a resumption of practice. Clive resisted at first, then gave in. As they walked out on to the field, he saw a car draw up on the road between the field and the church. A man got out, unfurling a black umbrella over his head.

'You lot carry on,' Clive said to the boys, tossing the ball on to the pitch.

The man was walking towards him. He was grey-haired, and Clive thought he recognized him. From the hospital, or perhaps a newspaper photograph. Then he remembered the story in the local newspaper about the surgeon who'd retired after having been sued for negligence. Charlie Fairhead had also talked about it at

99

the hospital, saying what a crime it was. But Clive couldn't remember his name.

'Mr King?' the man said as he drew level with Clive. 'Mr Clive King?'

'That's me.'

'I'm Ewart Plimmer. Would you mind if I had a word with you?'

'What did that man want, dad?' the boys asked him as he drove them home after the practice.

'There's a new job on offer working nights. He wanted to chat to me about it.'

'Are you going to take it?'

'You bet I am. For one thing, I'll earn more money, and that'll help me keep you pair in football boots.'

'We'll never see you if you work nights,' said Errol.

'Course you will. We'll switch the football practices to the evenings, and I'll be up by then. We'd have had to do that soon, anyway, when you're back at school. You'll see as much of me as before.'

Clive hoped so, anyway. The extra money involved in the job wouldn't really been as significant a factor as the opportunity to be occupied at nights rather than lying sleepless in his bed. And he'd always found Casualty work more interesting because there was plenty of variety – you never knew what you might be doing from one hour to the next. He'd gone into nursing because he wanted to help people, and casualty work also made him feel useful in a very direct sort of way.

It was raining heavily again, and Clive had the wipers on full. The boys were drawing shapes with their fingers on the misted-up windows. Then they started to squabble as Bobby rubbed out one of Errol's pictures.

'Cut it out, you two,' Clive said over his shoulder.

Then, through the smeared patch on the window, he thought he glimpsed Leah on the pavement.

He had turned the car into their road, and now he pulled up outside the house. Leah's mother was standing in the open doorway, a cardigan draped around her shoulders. She looked panic-stricken.

Clive climbed out and hurried across to her. Leah came running back up the pavement. She also looked distraught.

'I only went next door for five minutes,' she said frantically to him.

'And I wasn't in the bathroom long,' Lucy added.

'What's happened?' Clive wanted to know.

'All the doors were open when I came out,' Lucy said. 'I didn't hear a thing.'

'Five minutes,' said Leah. 'How could it happen in five minutes?'

She was peering desperately both ways down the street. Clive took her arm and said, 'How could *what* happen?'

'Your father,' she told him. 'He's gone wandering again, in his pyjamas.'

7

'How old are you, then?' Terry Breen asked Megan
Roach as they left the hospital at the end of their shift.

'Twenty-one,' Megan told him.

'No, seriously. I reckon about forty-five.'

'Very flattering. But you're wrong.'

'It was a nice cake,' Mandy Jennings remarked. 'I love
marzipan.'

'I'll send you some in the post,' Terry said eagerly to
her, trying to catch her eye.

'I didn't get to eat any of it,' Megan mused. 'You lot
scoffed it all.'

'At least we sang you Happy Birthday,' said Terry.

'If you can call it singing,' Megan said with a grin.

Still, she was pleased. She'd told no one at the hospital
that it was her birthday, but she'd been greeted by a
cluster of cards when she'd arrived at seven that morning.
Then, during their lunch break, Sister Morgan had
appeared with a birthday cake covered with white icing.
On its top had been embellished a silver hypodermic,
squirting out the blood-red words HAPPY BIRTHDAY,
MEGAN. The slightly ghoulish humour was typical of
nursing staff everywhere.

They walked down the road towards the bus stops. It
had rained earlier, and the street gleamed with water,
even though the sun was now shining once more.

'You going my way?' Terry was asking Mandy. They
were both first-year student nurses in their early twenties,

Terry a slightly gauche young man, Mandy a pretty blonde.

'No,' Mandy replied, looking a bit puzzled. 'I don't think so. We live on opposite sides of Holby, don't we?'

'Well,' said Terry, 'I could always make a detour if you wanted me to.'

'What would be the point of that?' Mandy said with innocent puzzlement, obviously failing to grasp what he was driving at.

Megan saw Terry beginning to blush. 'No point at all really,' he managed to say. 'I was just wondering.'

Oh the torments of young love, Megan thought to herself as Terry coughed to hide his embarrassment. He obviously fancied Mandy like mad, but she remained utterly immune to his charms.

A bus pulled up – Mandy's. With a blithe 'See you tomorrow', she climbed on board.

Terry stared after the bus as it pulled away, and Megan could see the yearning for romance in his eyes.

'She's pretty, isn't she?' Megan remarked.

'Yes,' Terry said emphatically, as though clutching at a conversational straw. 'Really, really pretty.' He glanced at Megan. 'Do you think it's me? I've been trying to, you know, well – '

'Ask her out?'

'Well, yes, eventually. But first I want to get her to, like, *notice* me. Only I can't get through to her somehow. Do you think it's me?'

Megan did not say that in her view Mandy was nice enough but a bit dim and self-absorbed; this was not what Terry wanted to hear. And in any case, it wasn't the whole problem.

'I mean,' Terry was saying, 'am I doing something *wrong*?'

The younger staff often sought her advice on personal matters, and she knew she was something of a mother-figure to them.

'Well,' she replied, 'you're not exactly Mr Tact. For one thing, you just don't ask women straight out how old they are.'

'No?'

'No – it's rude. And you're a bit too eager with her. You come on too strong. You have to try to be more subtle in getting her to notice you.'

'How?'

'That's really up to you. The thing to do is to show her you're interested without fawning all over her.'

'But how?' Terry insisted.

Megan tried to think. Terry and Mandy were a particularly difficult couple to try to pair off, and she didn't actually think that Terry had much hope. But she had to try to offer him some useful advice.

'Well,' she said desperately, 'be a bit more light-hearted with her.'

'I could tell her jokes,' Terry said instantly. 'I know a lot of them. Have you heard the one about the porcupine and the chimpanzee?'

'Not that one,' Megan said adamantly. That particular joke had been circulating the ward for the past week, and it was disgusting.

But Terry looked pleased at this possibility. His bus pulled in and he climbed on board.

'Thanks for your help,' he said from the platform as it pulled away. 'I'll make a list this evening.'

What have I done? Megan thought with a wry smile as the double-decker dwindled into the distance.

There was still no sign of her own bus. The boys were due home at four o'clock, and she had a dinner to cook for them. She'd stop off at the local supermarket and get some stewing steak. It was unlikely that her husband, Alf, would have surfaced yet.

A woman dressed in a tattered and stained overcoat came stumbling down the street, a bottle of sherry clutched in her hand. Her grey hair was matted and filthy, and she stared straight ahead with the fixed expression of the hopelessly drunk.

Megan would have done no more than glance at her had she not suddenly stumbled and lurched into her. The stench of alcohol was strong on her breath, as was the reek of her unwashed clothing. Megan had grabbed her arms to steady her, and then she saw her face. A shock of recognition passed through her.

'Alice,' she said. 'Alice Biley.'

The woman stared at her with bleary eyes. Her face remained slack of all expression.

'Don't you remember me? It's Megan. Megan Roach.'

The woman blinked, then hiccuped. Though she had not seen her in over twenty years, Megan had no doubt that this was her old friend from her student nurse days. They had trained together, been close. Alice had been a lively if somewhat nervous girl, an ex-Jehovah's Witness who had taken to nursing. Later their lives had separated and Megan had heard that she'd left nursing after having had a nervous breakdown precipitated by the death of a patient in her charge. She could hardly believe that this was what had become of her.

'Don't you know me, Alice?' she said again.

'Leave me alone,' came the reply. And the woman wrenched herself away, went hurrying off down the street.

A bus pulled in – the bus that would take her home. Megan wanted to run after her old friend, but already she was rushing across the road, dodging around the traffic, then disappearing down a sidestreet.

The people behind her were pressing forward, forcing her to climb on to the bus.

A beef stew was bubbling on the cooker while Megan washed up the pots and pans left over from the previous evening's meal. She made a lot of noise as she was doing so, banging the pots against the side of the aluminium sink while muttering under her breath: 'Ungrateful louts. Ought to give them bread and water for their supper, and perhaps then they'd start remembering things.'

Ten minutes earlier, her three sons had returned from the garage where they worked as mechanics, and she could hear them upstairs, laughing and squabbling over who was going to use the bathroom first. It was the same performance every evening. Meanwhile Alf was still fast asleep in bed.

'Ought to throw the lot of them out,' she murmured to herself. 'I get cards from my brothers and sisters, all the way from Ireland. But could they remember when they're in the same house as me? Came home empty-handed, without even a word. And Alf's forgotten as well – too busy sleeping. I'll ram a dishcloth up the exhaust of his taxi, she thought, and wash the boys' overalls in bleach. That'll teach 'em to take me for granted.'

Further laughter filtered down the stairs from the landing, and then she heard her eldest, Paul, shout, 'Mum, can you come up here a moment.'

She pretended not to hear, but he shouted again.

'I'm cooking!' she shouted back. 'Someone has to do the work around here.'

'It's important, mum,' called Bernard, her youngest.

Giving a long-suffering sigh, she removed her hands

from the sink and dried them on the tea-towel. Then she went out into the hallway.

There was no sign of the boys on the landing.

'Where are you?' she called up the stairs. 'I haven't got time for silly games!'

'We're in your bedroom,' Paul replied. 'Dad's not here.'

She put one foot on the stairs. 'What do you mean?'

'Has he gone out?' This was her second son, Mark.

'Of course he hasn't. He's in bed.'

'No, he isn't.'

She climbed the stairs, knowing that they were messing around with her, and determined to give them a piece of her mind. The bathroom door was open, and she could see a tide-mark right around the bath where the boys had neglected to clean it after soaping the muck and grease from themselves. That was another thing she was going to give them a piece of her mind about.

The curtains were still drawn in the bedroom and it was gloomy inside. Paul, Mark and Bernard were standing beside the bed, but there was no sign of Alf, just a pile of rumpled clothes.

Megan knew that he couldn't have gone out without her hearing him. She glared suspiciously at the boys, all of whom were freshly laundered in jeans, shirts and sweaters.

'What's going on?' she demanded.

They all immediately protested their innocence.

'Alf?' she said. 'Alf, where are you?'

'The window's locked,' said Paul, 'I checked it, so he couldn't have got out that way.'

'Very funny', said Megan.

'And I've looked under all our beds,' said Bernard. 'Unless he's turned into a pair of slippers, he's not there.'

107

'Hilarious.'

Bernard was standing beside the wardrobe with his hands behind his back. Suddenly there was a creaking sound, and the wardrobe door opened, startling Megan. Out stepped a figure swathed in white, holding something on which glowed a candle.

Megan almost fainted with surprise until the boys burst into a cracked rendition of 'Happy Birthday to You'. At the same time she realized that the figure was Alf, with a white sheet draped over his shoulders. He was holding a birthday cake in the shape of a nurse's hat. It was decorated with the number fifty-two in red icing.

'Many happy returns, sunshine,' said Alf, beaming. And then he planted a big kiss on her forehead.

'You could have given me a heart attack,' Megan said when the singing had subsided.

'Don't give us that,' said Alf. 'We all know you like a bit of a fright. That's why we thought we'd catch you unawares. Are you going to blow out the candle?'

She blew.

When they went downstairs, Alf gave her her present – a bunch of keys.

'What are these for?' she asked.

'Come round the back,' Alf told her.

Their terraced house gave out on a narrow lane dominated on both sides by custom-built garages. Outside the back gate next to Alf's taxi stood a Morris Traveller, painted cherry and cream.

'It's yours,' Alf told her. 'I bought it off a friend, and it's in good nick. The boys have given it a complete overhaul and a respray.'

'I can see that,' Megan said. 'It looks like an ice-cream van.'

'We made sure it was striking,' Paul said, 'so that other

drivers would know you were coming and be able to take evasive action.'

She prodded him in the ribs with her elbow; it was a family joke that she wasn't the best of drivers, though in fact she drove perfectly well.

'We thought of putting chimes in as well,' added Mark. 'Though maybe a siren would be better – then everyone would be able to get out of the way in time.'

It was his turn to receive a prod in the ribcage. She glared at Bernard, expecting some quip from him. But he backed away, holding out his hands as if to fend her off. 'I didn't say a word.'

'I'm just waiting for your contribution.'

'Well,' he said, unable to resist it, 'I suggested a megaphone on top, broadcasting warning messages. Something along the lines of – ' he broke into song ' – Whoa-oh, here she comes, she's the man-eater!'

Megan chased him around the car, cornered him and tickled him until he squirmed.

Despite all the banter, she was touched. Her old car had finally expired a month ago, and she had been getting the bus into the hospital or having Alf give her a lift if it was convenient. But Alf had evidently not forgotten that a Morris Traveller had been her first – and favourite – car. It was well over twenty years since she had driven one, and she couldn't wait to get behind the steering wheel.

'There's more inside,' Alf said to her.

On the front two seats were a number of gift-wrapped packages and envelopes. Opening the door, she took them out.

Alf had also bought her a two-pound box of Thornton's Continental chocolates; she had always had a sweet tooth. From Paul were three video cassettes of *Psycho, The*

Abominable Dr Phibes and *The Incredible Shrinking Man*; though she hated unnecessary blood and gore, she had always enjoyed a good suspense or horror film. Mark's present comprised a simple envelope inside which were two tickets for free perms at her favourite hairdressers; it was another family joke that she had her hair done so often that she needed a season ticket. And Bernard had bought her Trivial Pursuit, reflecting the whole family's enjoyment of all sorts of table games from jigsaws to Monopoly.

'I thought you'd all forgotten,' Megan told them. 'I was cursing you black and blue.'

She insisted on giving them all a kiss in turn, even though the boys tended to find this sort of thing rather sloppy. Paul was twenty-four, Mark twenty and Bernard eighteen, and they were all tall boys like their father, with a practical bent. Cars seemed to run in the family's blood, Alf having been a night taxi-driver since before they'd married, the boys having had their heads inside bonnets before they were actually old enough to drive. Now they more or less ran the garage where they had been taken on as apprentices straight from school.

'Well,' she said, 'I'd better go and get our dinner ready.'

Alf shook his head. 'Not tonight – we're dining out.'

'But I've made a stew.'

'It'll keep till tomorrow. I've booked a table at *The Taj Mahal*. You're driving us there in the Traveller.'

'We've got our crash helmets,' said Paul.

'And our rabbit's feet,' added Mark.

'And a big bottle of valium,' concluded Bernard.

Alf Roach studied his wife across the kitchen table. She met his eye and he winked at her. She winked back and grinned.

Trivial Pursuit was spread out in front of them, and Mark was asking Bernard a question about what pop star had married someone else in 1970. Alf and Megan exchanged wry grins, knowing that they had no hope of winning the game. Bernard had bought the Baby Boomer edition, designed for the generation which had grown up in the 1960s and '70s, and filled with questions about pop music and celebrities whom they had never heard of. The boys had almost filled up their wheels, whereas he and Megan had only one triangle each in theirs. But it hadn't spoiled the evening at all.

They had returned from the restaurant an hour earlier, having had an excellent meal. Megan was, as ever, in good spirits, warm and good-natured, and tolerant of their sons' continual ribbing. The Three Stooges, Alf sometimes called them since they so often behaved like a comedy act. It still amazed him that all three of them had remained close to both himself and Megan. They were a truly happy family.

Most of this was Megan's doing. Like any other family, they had had their problems over the years, but Megan had always had the uncanny knack of sensing when things were going wrong at an early stage and taking steps to prevent them from getting worse. This was what had made her an excellent wife and mother, and Alf was pretty sure that it also made her an excellent nurse. Had she had the ambition, she could have been a Sister or a Staff Nurse by now, but she seemed quite content to continue as an ordinary SEN. I'm happy in my work, she would tell him; I don't want any more responsibility, what with having to look after you lot as well.

In almost thirty years of marriage, Alf had never been less than content and had never so much as looked at another woman. This kind of contentment and faithfulness was rare, he knew, and he cherished it. His only regret was that he and Megan didn't have more time to spend together. With him always working nights and sleeping late into the afternoons, he only got to see her for any proper length of time when she was also on the night shift.

'Dad,' said Paul, offering him the dice. 'It's your turn.'

Alf glanced at Megan, then said, 'I think me and your mother'll retire gracefully and leave you three to battle it out.'

'Things can change fast in this game. You could still win.'

'Not with questions about yellow polka-dot bikinis and Tiny Tim. I thought he was an elephant. We're going to go and put a film on the video.'

'I'll come too,' said Mark, who was trailing his other brothers in the game. 'I've never seen *Psycho*.'

'No you won't,' Alf said firmly. 'Me and your mother are going to have a couple of hours to ourselves. *Alone*, in the living room with the telly.'

'Just like a couple of teenagers,' Paul said, grinning. 'Want us to fetch you a bag of popcorn and some lollipops?'

'I'll fetch you a thick ear if you disturb us before the film's over. And that'll be midnight, when I'm off to work.'

'What do we do when we've finished the game?' asked Bernard.

'You'll think of something.'

He and Megan went through the living room. Alf slotted *Psycho* into the video machine, and he and Megan settled down on the sofa for a cuddle.

'You're quiet,' he said to her as the credits began to appear.

'I was thinking about an old friend,' she told him. 'Alice Biley. Remember her?'

Alf frowned. 'I don't think so.'

'Maybe you never met. We trained together as nurses, and we used to be very close. I bumped into her again today for the first time in years.'

He peered at her. 'And?'

'She's a down-and-out. Pouring cheap sherry down her neck and wandering the streets like a hobo. Filthy. She didn't seem to recognize me.'

He waited, knowing she would tell him more.

'She had a breakdown after a patient committed suicide on her. Apparently it was pretty messy – blood-soaked sheets and all that. So she gave up nursing and disappeared from sight. I haven't seen her in years, but I never thought she'd end up in such a state. She was always a bit highly strung, but she used to be such a smart young woman, very fussy about her appearance. Took it all too personally, though. She'd been very religious, and I think she was one of those people who were always finding ways to make themselves feel guilty about things.'

'Did you talk to her?'

'She ran away from me – I didn't really get a chance.'

The opening credits were appearing on the screen. Alf was holding the automatic control, and he touched the volume button, turning down the sound.

'If only I knew where she was living,' Megan said. 'I could go and visit her, find out how she is. If she *has* a place, that is.'

Alf didn't really know what to say. Megan sighed and shrugged.

'I suppose there's not much use in worrying about it,' she said.

'You can't be Florence Nightingale to everyone, pet.'

She peered up at him, then grinned; it was his standard advice to her whenever she was in danger of letting her protective instincts overwhelm her. She glanced at the screen and said, 'It's started. Turn it up.'

He did so. Soon he felt her relaxing against him as she became engrossed in the story. *Psycho* was one of her favourite films, he knew, and she never tired of watching it.

He put an arm around her waist, and she snuggled up to him. Then Alf heard a sniggering behind them before Mark's voice said:

'No funny business in the back row!'

The three boys were all peering through the serving hatch in the wall between the kitchen and the living room. Alf was about to fling a newspaper at them when the doorbell rang.

He went out into the hallway and opened the front door.

'Mr Roach?' said the man with grey hair who was standing there.

'That's me.'

'Is your wife in? I'm Ewart Plimmer, from the City Hospital. I was wondering if I could have a chat with her.'

8

Duffy was dreaming that she was in Venice – or somewhere resembling Venice, since there were canals and bridges and gondolas everywhere. There was also Blackpool tower, but in the dream she took no notice of this but instead was caught up in the romance of a strange and exotic place.

She stood on a cobbled embankment beside the canal's edge, waiting for an approaching gondola to dock and take her on board. The gondolier was dressed in a matador's costume of black and silver, and although she couldn't see his face under the shadow of his cap, she was sure he would be handsome, the man of her dreams.

Veils of mist hung very romantically over the water, and above the sky was blue, the sun warm on her head. This is the life, she thought as the gondola drew near. Overhead, seagulls swooped and cawed.

From nearby, she could hear laughter, though there didn't appear to be anyone else around. The sun was now very hot on her face and forehead, while the clothes she was wearing – she could not actually see them – suddenly felt very heavy.

The sounds of laughter grew louder just as the gondola came abreast of her, and at last she was able to see the man in the matador's suit properly. He had black curly hair and lamb-chop sideboards, and his suit was open to the belly, revealing a gold medallion which hung from a chain on his matted chest. He looked like a Teddy Boy gone to seed – not her type at all.

'Hello, darling,' he said to her in a pronounced West Country accent. 'Would you like me to show you a good time?'

She might have known it – a right prat. But something was compelling her to step aboard the gondola even as the laughter around her grew still louder and she began to feel even hotter under the sun. As she was climbing aboard she stumbled, overturned the gondola and plunged both her and the gondolier into the water.

The shock of this caused her to wake up abruptly. She was lying under a blue sky, with the sun blazing down on her face. But she was also still in her bed.

It took a few moments before she was able to orientate herself. She knew that she should be in her room in the nurses' home, a modern tower block which rose to twenty storeys near Northville Park and the motorway. But she wasn't there – she seemed to be out in the open. Then it dawned on her that her bed had been dragged halfway out of her room so that she was lying half out on the balcony window, in the full heat of the August sun.

No wonder she was hot. No wonder, in her dress, she had felt weighted down by her clothes – they were actually bedclothes. And now she realized that the laughter she had heard in the dream was continuing, coming from inside her room.

She sat up. Eileen and Kate were peering around the glass doors at her, giggling.

'I was dreaming,' she said. 'About being in Venice. It had Blackpool tower in it.'

'Have you ever been to Venice?' Kate asked.

'No,' said Duffy. 'But I've been to Blackpool.'

'Are you going to get up?' said Eileen.

'What time is it?'

116

'After eleven. We're supposed to be going to the fair today.'

She nodded, remembering, then stifled a yawn.

'We tried tweaking your toes,' Eileen said, 'and sprinkling water on your face. But you were dead to the world.'

'I hate mornings. You know that. So whose bright idea was it to drag me out here to wake me up?'

'It needed both of us to move the bed,' said Kate.

'Then both of you can have one of these.'

And Duffy hurled a pillow at each of them.

They caught a bus out to the fair, which was being held on Abbotswood Down, not far from the suspension bridge over the gorge. It was the perfect day for it, as hot and bright as in her dream. Duffy was always fantasizing about visiting far-off romantic places and meeting handsome young men who would sweep her off her feet. This annoyed her, because in her real life she considered herself practical and down-to-earth. Well, *reasonably* down-to-earth. At least she was able to tell a prat from a mile off.

Born in Holby, Duffy was twenty-two, and she had just completed her training as a State Registered Nurse. The hardest part of the job as far as she was concerned was getting up early in the mornings when she was working days. Afternoons she could cope with, and nights were even better since she had always functioned best between midnight and dawn. She loved nursing not out of any great idealistic motives but because she enjoyed the companionship and variety of the work.

Eileen shared a room with her, and Kate was just across the corridor in the nurses' home; the three of them had become close during their training. Eileen was an Irish Catholic from Belfast, Kate the daughter of a

117

Conservative MP in Hertfordshire whose strong right-wing views – especially on the subject of the NHS – now appalled her. Their wildly different backgrounds somehow helped them to get along together even better, and they called themselves Snap, Crackle and Pop when they were in a frivolous mood.

The fair was in full flow when they arrived, crowds munching toffee apples and hot dogs and milling around side shows, helter skelters, merry-go-rounds, go-carts and dodgems. Duffy wasn't able to resist hurling balls at pyramids of battered tin cans; she spent £1.20 winning an ashtray which couldn't have been worth more than 30p. Eileen then demonstrated her prowess with an airgun, knocking off several ping-pong balls which were perched on jets of water. She won a cuddly toy which looked like a mutant variety of Kermit the Frog. Then Kate threw darts at playing cards until she finally came away with a vase that caused all three of them to fall about laughing at its close resemblance to a urine bottle.

They lunched on hot dogs and candy floss, then attempted to get the better of a few Space Invaders machines, without success. They stood in front of fairground mirrors, the squat Eileen suddenly looking willowy in one which elongated her reflection, the tall and slender Kate being flattened to Bunteresque proportions by hers. Duffy, who was of average height and build with fair hair swept back from her face, grimaced cheekily at a mirror which distorted her girl-next-door attractiveness into squashed, chimp-like features.

'Hello, darling,' said a voice behind her. 'Give us a banana.'

Standing nearby were three boys in their late teens, dressed in denims and cowboy boots. They were blatantly eyeing up Duffy, Eileen and Kate. Duffy exchanged glances with her two friends. Though no words were exchanged, they all agreed with their expressions that they weren't interested, so they walked on without responding.

'Fancy a go on the dodgems?' one of the boys called after them.

'We're nuns,' Eileen said without looking back.

Duffy noticed a stall tucked away in one corner.

'Look!' she said, pointing. The sign above the stall read MADAME NATASHA, FORTUNE TELLER.

'Oh no you don't,' Kate and Eileen said in unison, trying to drag her away.

'Come on,' she said to them. 'Let's give it a go.'

'What is it with you?' Eileen asked. 'You're always getting your horoscope charted or your palm read or your tea-leaves inspected. By now you should know exactly what's going to happen to you in the future.'

'No,' said Duffy, 'it's always changing. What you do today affects what happens tomorrow.'

'Very profound,' Kate said drily.

'You're just sceptical because you're a Scorpio,' Duffy said confidently, though she wasn't quite able to remember if this was exactly right. Her keenest interest was in the Zodiac, but it was a complicated subject and sometimes she got the details a bit muddled.

'I don't think you should be messing around with that stuff,' Eileen insisted. 'What will be, will be, and it's better not to know.'

'You're just saying that because you're a Catholic.'

'I'm not one any more. Haven't been to confession in years.'

'Well, it's the same thing. Once a Catholic, always a Catholic. And you're a Libra, which makes you cautious. Because they can never make up their minds about anything, they prefer to bury their heads in the sand.'

'Come here often?' called one of the boys, who were still trailing them.

'At least we'd get out of *their* way,' Duffy said.

'*I'm* going on The Whip,' Kate announced.

'Me, too,' said Eileen.

But Duffy couldn't let the opportunity pass.

'I'll see you back here in twenty minutes,' she said. And then she hastened off towards the stall.

A somewhat moth-eaten scarlet drape hung over the entrance, and Duffy pushed it aside. Beyond it was a small booth in which sat an adolescent boy, picking his nose. He made no attempt to extract his finger when he saw Duffy, but instead probed even deeper into his nostril.

'Is Madame Natasha free?' Duffy asked, for want of anything better to say.

'Yep,' said the boy, finally removing his finger. 'It's a pound.'

Duffy rummaged in her purse and produced a coin which she put on the counter. The boy snatched it away with amazing speed.

There was another curtain behind the booth, and Duffy could hear a woman coughing behind it.

'In there?' she asked, pointing.

'Yep,' said the boy, his finger already probing his other nostril.

Madame Natasha's cubicle was lit by a single candle, so that it was gloomy inside. The air was thick with acrid cigarette smoke, and Duffy edged her way forward cautiously as her eyes adjusted to the dimness.

Suitably gypsy-like in appearance, Madame Natasha was seated at a small table draped with a black cloth. There was a crystal ball in front of her.

'Take a seat,' she told Duffy in a hoarse voice with a distinct London accent.

Duffy sat.

'Give me your hands.'

Obediently, Duffy put her hands across the table, and Madame Natasha took them in her own. The fortune teller's fingers were stained beech-brown with nicotine, and her skin was hard and dry, like autumn leaves.

'You have a thoughtful face,' the woman said, peering at her across the table. She wore a dark green shawl over her shoulders, and her greying hair was drawn back into a severe bun. 'You are interested in other people and you have a sensitive heart.'

'I'm a nurse,' Duffy said.

Madame Natasha nodded sagely. 'You care for others, but sometimes feel neglected yourself.'

This was true, Duffy realized, and she nodded fractionally.

'You are unhappy with your love-life.'

Again Duffy nodded. 'My boyfriend, Caesar – that's his nickname – he takes me a bit for granted. I think he may be getting fed up of me.'

Duffy had been going out with Caesar – whose nickname came from the fact that his middle name was Julius – for almost a year. But he was often late for their dates and seemed to prefer to go drinking with his friends rather than see her. He worked as a book-keeper in an estate agent's office, and she had begun to suspect that he fancied one of the secretaries there.

Madame Natasha was now peering into the crystal ball while continuing to hold one of Duffy's hands.

'Can you see what's going to happen between us?' Duffy asked. 'Are we going to be all right?'

'I foresee difficulties and possibly a separation. Much

121

depends on your own actions. You must examine your own feelings carefully and make no hasty decisions.'

This sounded slightly vague to Duffy, but then she knew better than to expect clear-cut answers and predictions from fortune-telling; it was, after all, an art not a science, and much depended on the unpredictability of human behaviour.

'I foresee great changes in your life,' Madame Natasha said, peering intently at the crystal ball in which Duffy could see nothing but trapped bubbles of air.

'When?' she asked.

'Perhaps soon. Perhaps very soon. There is an older man.'

'An older man?'

'I can see him only faintly. He will be involved in these changes which will take place.'

'Do you know who he might be?'

'He could be a member of your family . . .'

'My dad's dead.'

'. . . or he may be someone with whom you will become involved professionally. He is a man whose judgement it will be wise to trust.'

Duffy was excited at the prospect of this new development, especially since she had felt that her life was becoming a bit boring of late.

'Can you tell me any more?' she asked.

Madame Natasha shook her head slowly. 'The mists are closing over, and there is no more to be seen. But there can be no doubt – a new and exciting phase will open in your life very soon.'

It became clear to Duffy that the consultation was over, for Madame Natasha had just produced a packet of Capstan Full Strength from the folds of her shawl. She lit one up, inhaled, began coughing fiercely. Duffy waited patiently for the fit to subside.

'Beware of sharp instruments,' the fortune teller said abruptly.

Duffy immediately thought of needles and scalpels.

'I can tell you no more,' Madame Natasha said. 'But I had a flash that a sharp instrument may be of danger to you in the near future. Otherwise, everything will work out for the best and you will be fulfilled by any changes which will occur.'

Though she had spent little more than five minutes in the cubicle, Duffy was satisfied. Excitement was promised in her life, and the hint of danger was only to be expected if she was going to be taking risks or moving into unfamiliar territory. Better that than boredom.

Thanking the fortune teller, she departed, Madame Natasha's coughing following her as she went. In the booth the boy was rolling something between his fingers. Duffy hurried past him, out into the fresh air.

Kate and Eileen had been cornered by the three boys near The Whip. Eileen looked a little green in the gills, while Kate was attempting to fend off the boys' clumsy advances.

'Where's your mate?' one of them was asking her.

'Right behind you,' Kate said.

He spun around, then grinned at Duffy. 'Hello, darling. What's your name then?'

'Snap,' said Duffy.

'I'm Crackle,' added Kate, 'and she's Pop.'

Kate indicated Eileen, who was leaning against the wicker fence surrounding The Whip, looking distinctly out of sorts. She was clutching Kermit the Frog to her breast as if her life depended on it.

123

'I'm Atila the Hun,' said the boy, still staring at Duffy. 'What's your real name?'

'Doris,' Duffy said. 'Doris Duffin.'

'Very funny.'

She was, in fact, telling the truth. Her mother had christened her Doris, a name she had always hated and never used. She was Duffy to everyone else who knew her.

'What's in the bag?' another of the boys asked Kate.

Earlier Kate had put the vase she had won in a brown paper bag.

'You wouldn't believe me if I told you,' she said.

'What do you do, then?' asked the third of the boys.

'Do?' said Kate.

'For a living. Or are you on the dole, like us?'

'We're nurses,' said Duffy.

'Ah,' said the boy who had obviously taken a fancy to her. 'I've got a pain down here.' His hand went down the front of his jeans. 'Would you have a look at it for me?'

'Don't need to,' Duffy retorted. 'I'll tell you what to do – soak it in cold water for an hour.'

'I feel terrible,' Eileen moaned.

'Sounds like she needs a doctor,' one of the boys said, grinning.

'She felt a bit sick on The Whip,' Kate said for Duffy's benefit. 'I think we'd better get her to the toilets.'

'We'll come with you,' said one of the boys.

'Don't be daft,' Kate said. 'But you can do us a favour – hold this for me, till we come back.'

She offered him the paper bag which held the vase; the bag had been screwed up at its top. He took it from her, obviously convinced that they would have to return to reclaim it.

Duffy and Kate led Eileen off to the women's toilets, a

caravan which stood behind the Ghost Train, out of sight of the boys. As they approached it, Eileen said, 'I'm beginning to feel better already.'

'Good,' said Kate, 'then let's get out of here, shall we?'

Eileen nodded. 'I've had enough – especially with those three starting to pester us.'

The bus stop was just along the road, and even as she stared, Duffy saw a bus approaching in the distance.

'What about your vase?' she asked Kate.

'You can forget that. They're going to have a shock when they unscrew the top of the paper bag.'

They hurried towards the bus stop, Kate and Eileen grinning.

'Why?' Duffy wanted to know. 'What's wrong with it?'

'There's nothing wrong with it,' said Kate. 'It's what's inside it.'

Duffy glanced at Eileen, who was looking a little shame-faced.

'You didn't?' she said to her.

Eileen nodded. 'I got sick while we were on The Whip. Kate passed me the vase – it was the only thing to hand.'

'Then those three clowns stopped us just as we got off,' Kate added, 'before we could get rid of it.'

'And you've left them holding it?'

Kate merely grinned.

'That's disgusting,' Duffy said.

'I know,' Kate replied as the bus drew up and they climbed on board. 'But it's funny, too, isn't it?'

'She told me an older man's going to change my life soon,' Duffy was explaining to Kate and Eileen after their arrival home. Duffy and Kate were in the bedroom, and Kate had removed a tobacco tin and some cigarette papers from under the coffee table, where they had been sellotaped.

'She probably means your bank manager,' Eileen said from the kitchen, where she was making coffee. 'Getting a bit worried about your overdraft, isn't he?'

Duffy ignored the remark. 'She also said that I've got to be careful of sharp instruments.'

Kate was licking the cigarette paper. She smiled. 'Judging by the way that kid stuffed his hand down the front of his jeans, she should have warned you about blunt instruments.'

Duffy smiled back. 'What a trio. They were about as subtle as a punch in the nose.'

'Well, I left them with a present that they won't forget in a hurry.'

'Did you really?'

'Of course she didn't,' said Eileen, carrying the mugs of coffee through from the kitchen. 'You didn't think I was really sick on The Whip, did you?'

Duffy looked at her, then back at Kate.

'She's just trying to cover up for herself,' Kate said.

'As if I'd do such a thing,' Eileen insisted.

Both of them were grinning, so Duffy didn't know who to believe. She was lying on the bed, and she picked up two pillows and hurled them at her friends. The first narrowly missed the coffees, the second hit Kate on the back of the head.

'It's the truth!' Kate insisted.

'She's having you on,' Eileen said, equally adamantly.

Duffy decided to give up on them. Perhaps she'd never know what had really happened. She watched Kate spread tobacco on the cigarette papers, then take a small polythene bag from the tin. Inside it was what looked like an Oxo cube. It was, in fact, cannabis resin – a lump of

126

Lebanese Gold which Kate had been given by her boy-friend, James, the previous day. James worked for a reputable firm of chartered accountants, but this didn't prevent him from having access to a steady supply of dope.

Duffy did not smoke much, but she found that the occasional joint relaxed her in a way that alcohol couldn't do. She wasn't interested in any other drugs, and she only smoked when she was not on duty.

Kate was about to crumble some of the cube over the line of tobacco when the doorbell rang.

'It's probably Sally,' Kate remarked. 'She said she might drop in.'

Sally was Kate's room-mate. Carrying her mug, Eileen went through into the living room and opened the door.

'Ah,' said a man's voice. 'Coffee. Splendid.'

Eileen simply gaped at him.

'Is there a D. Duffin here?' he asked.

Immediately Kate and Duffy began hiding the evidence of the joint under the mattress. Through the open door, Duffy glimpsed a man with silvery hair and an age-weathered face.

The older man, she thought immediately, that the fortune-teller told me about.

'Do you mean Duffy?' said Eileen, stalling for time.

'Yes. That would be the person.'

Eileen glanced back over her shoulder into the bed-room. All the incriminating evidence had been removed. As she ushered the man inside, Duffy rose and stood to attention. Something told her that the new phase in her life was about to begin.

9

When the call came, Clive was having a secret scotch in the living room, and he only just managed to hide the glass before Leah appeared.

'It's the hospital,' she said, grim-faced. 'They've had someone in who answers to his description.'

'Dead?' He could hardly say the word.

She nodded.

The phone was in the hallway. He picked it up, identified himself, then listened to the gory details. A body of a black man in his late sixties had been found in Holby Docks, dressed in a long overcoat over pyjamas. Blue-striped pyjamas. Exactly like the ones his father had been wearing. He knew then that it was all over.

He put the phone down, feeling numb. For three days he had frantically driven around the city, searching everywhere for his father, but to no avail. The police had been alerted and he had been given leave-of-absence from the hospital. He hadn't slept at all since his father's disappearance, and from the start he had been convinced that it would all end badly.

'They want me to go to the hospital and identify the body,' he said to Leah.

'I'll come with you.'

He shook his head. 'No. I'd rather do this myself. Where are the boys?'

'Out in the garden.'

'Don't say anything to them until I get back.'

'Do you think it's him?'

'I'm certain of it.'

Chopin's polonaises. As played by Glenn Gould. What could be a better way of relaxing after a hectic day?

Ewart sat in his armchair, his feet up, a scotch and water in his hand. It was the first drink he'd had in several days, and it was heavily diluted with water. He didn't need alcohol to blunt the edges of his daily existence any more; he had more than enough to keep him occupied.

He had closed the music room door behind him, and now he felt comfortably sealed off from the rest of the world for a few hours. He'd spent most of the day at the hospital, checking the facilities of the new annex. There was only a week to go before the new night shift started, and much still needed to be done. But the cubicles in the annex had been converted for casualty use, and the crash room would be ready in time for real emergencies. All in all, things were going well.

Professionally, at least. In his private life, things were much greyer. Ros had still not returned home, and she had phoned him the previous day to say that Madge was still feeling poorly and that she intended staying on in Swindon for a few more days at least. Ewart suspected that Madge was not really unwell at all, but he hadn't pressed the matter. Once again the conversation had been stiff and awkward, though Ros had asked him if he was getting on with the back garden. He had been so relieved by this conversational lifeline that he'd launched into an account of how well things were going and what plans he had for his vegetable patch. In fact he'd done nothing but cleared a small area of weeds. Tomorrow, he promised himself, I'll have a real attack on it, tidy it all up before she gets home.

Ewart became aware of a low buzzing which he thought at first was coming from the stereo. He sat up in alarm, then realized that it was the doorbell.

It had been dusk when Ewart had entered his music room, but he always lost track of time when he was in there, and so he was not surprised to find that it was pitch-black outside. His watch showed ten-thirty. He opened the door, and found Joyce standing in the porch.

She was dressed in a black gaberdine overcoat with the collar up, even though it wasn't particularly cold. In her right hand she held a small white china jug.

'This is stupid,' she said to him, 'but I've run out of milk. Could you spare a drop?'

'Of course,' Ewart said. 'Come in.'

'I must be going scatter-brained,' she said as Ewart led her through the house to the kitchen. 'I went out shopping this morning and got all my groceries, but I completely forgot about milk. It's not like me at all. I was about to have a hot chocolate to take to bed with me when I realized it was all gone.'

Ewart opened his fridge door. There was a pint and a half of milk inside.

'No Marvel either,' Joyce was saying. 'I usually keep some dried milk in stock, just in case. It's really stupid of me.'

Ewart took the full pint from the fridge and offered it to her. 'You can take this.'

'Oh, I don't need all that.'

'Neither do I tonight. And there'll be a delivery in the morning. I don't drink much, and I've been pouring the stuff away in the past few days because it's gone off.'

She took the bottle from him, peered quickly around. 'Ros not back yet?'

'No, not yet. Still at her sister's.'

Joyce nodded understandingly, though once again Ewart was pretty sure she had known full well that Ros hadn't returned.

'Donald's away as well,' she said.

'Oh?'

'Bahrain. For two months.'

Ewart nodded, only now noticing that she appeared to be wearing a frilly nightdress immediately under her overcoat.

'Gets lonely, doesn't it?' she said. 'When you're on your own a lot.'

'I suppose it would.'

'You're not missing Ros, then?'

'Well . . .'

'I know what you mean. Sometimes absence doesn't make the heart grow fonder, does it? It just makes you realize that you're not really missing a person as much as you thought you would. Sometimes, anyway. I often wonder about me and Donald. Whether we should really have got married. You know?'

She was smiling at him, her eyes forthright somehow. For the first time he realized that she was an attractive. woman. Age had treated her more kindly than Ros, and yet there was a slightly haunted, almost pleading, look in her eyes.

'It's difficult,' Ewart said blandly, not knowing what else to say.

'We all need closeness,' she said. 'Someone to share a few private moments with, don't we?'

Ewart was pretty sure that this was an invitation; he was pretty sure that it would be perfectly possible for him to take her in his arms and kiss her. She was waiting for it. And then one thing would lead to another.

'That's nice music,' she said, referring to the piano sounds drifting through from the music room.

'It's Chopin,' Ewart said.

'Lovely. You have a big record collection, don't you?'

I can't go through with this, Ewart thought. *I don't want to.* For Ros's sake, and for my own.

Joyce had moved subtly closer to him. He could smell her violet perfume.

'Well,' he said awkwardly, 'it's past my bed-time. Don't worry about returning the milk – it's on me.'

Joyce blinked, as if she had suddenly been awoken from a hypnotic trance. Ewart thought he saw a flicker of disappointment in her features, but then she mustered her composure.

'Yes,' she said briskly, 'thanks very much. I'm sorry I had to disturb you.'

She was already heading back through the house towards the front door. Ewart pursued her, suddenly feeling as if he was the one who had done something embarrassing.

'Good night,' she said, hurrying through the doorway, looking straight ahead.

'Good night,' he called after her, watching her disappear very quickly down the pathway.

He closed the door behind him, and only then did he realize that he was holding his breath. He exhaled heavily, then shook his head. Perhaps he had imagined it all; Joyce had not actually done or said anything improper, but he was pretty sure that it had been in the air. Why had he put her off? Not because he didn't find her attractive in a purely physical sense. No, he'd done so for the very reason that he had actually been tempted to be unfaithful to Ros. And that would have been the final straw.

He switched off the stereo and swallowed another mouthful of his drink. The telephone rang.

He did not move. His first thought was that the caller would be Joyce, ringing from her own home to apologize or clear the air. But that was an absurd idea, he decided. It was probably Ros, who hadn't rung all day. But he didn't want to speak to her just at this moment.

The phone kept ringing and Ewart stood there, his glass clutched tightly in his hand. Then he snatched up the receiver and said, 'Hello?'

'Mr Plimmer?'

'Yes.'

'It's Clive King. I'm afraid I've got a problem.'

Charlie was leaning against the bar of the club, watching the group on stage. The club was suitably cavernous in appearance, with dim lighting and a low roof that trapped all the heat and smoke in the place. Charlie was sweating. He drained his glass of shandy, ordered a refill, lit a cigarette.

'Not bad, are they?' said the man standing next to him. His name was Derek, and Charlie had a nodding acquaintance with him.

'They're all right,' Charlie said without enthusiasm. The four-piece band was blasting out a kind of post-punk version of 'Route 66', all vibrant guitars and flailing drums. They were young, Charlie thought – frighteningly young. Made him feel positively middle-aged.

The band's name was The Disaster Area, and the lead guitarist, a gangly nineteen-year-old named Chip, was Liz's nephew. She had dragged Charlie along to the club for the group's first gig in Holby, and he would have to try to think of something complimentary to say about them afterwards without actually lying. Liz herself had

133

once sung in a band during the '70s. Like many other groups of the time, they had had high expectations but had never quite made it.

Now The Disaster Area launched into one of their own compositions, delicately entitled 'Up Yours'. The acoustics were poor, and Charlie couldn't make out any of the lyrics. It's probably just as well, he thought. I've become a Boring Old Fart.

But he knew what was really bothering him. Liz had still not come to a decision over the job with City Sound in London, and for the last several days she had declared a moratorium on the subject, refusing to discuss it. This had made Charlie somewhat tetchy – he liked things out in the open. But at the same time he felt unable to offer Liz any constructive advice or support, and so they were in a kind of limbo. Not the best sort of situation when you were the impatient type.

Since arriving at the club, he hadn't actually seen Liz. She was backstage, helping out with the roadies. He reckoned that she missed the touring life more than she would admit.

The song came to an end, and for a moment there was silence. The club was packed with people, though the audience was parsimonious in its applause. Chip approached one of the microphones.

'Now,' he said, 'we'd like to introduce a special guest vocalist who some of you might remember from the Stone Age – Liz Coulson!'

Charlie was not entirely surprised to see Liz walk out on to the stage, all done up in black leather and fishnet gloves; she had dropped a hint that she might be performing beforehand.

'Hey,' said Derek, 'that's your missus, isn't it?'

134

'We live together,' Charlie replied. Somehow the statement seemed tentative, provisional.

Liz didn't bother with any introductions, for already the band was thundering into the opening riff of 'You Really Got Me'. Liz snatched the microphone from its stand and went strutting across the stage.

Her performance was much like the ones he remembered from the past – full of sound and fury. Liz had a strong if not exceptional voice, and she used it to good effect, half shouting out the lyrics as she strode up and down the narrow stage with The Disaster Area rampaging musically behind her.

'You Really Got Me' was followed by Talking Heads' 'Psycho Killer', and then the Stones' 'Let's Spend The Night Together'. Charlie, still standing under the yellow light of the bar, felt that Liz's eyes were fixed on him as she sang this last song, every word meant for him.

The set came to an end with this, but the audience were suitably enthusiastic, so the group returned to play an encore.

Suddenly the frenetic mood of the earlier songs vanished with a slower and gentler backing. Charlie recognized the song even before Liz started her vocals: it was The Beatles' 'Help'.

Once again Charlie stood there, feeling as if she was singing just for him. Whether the song was meant as an affirmation of their relationship or as a plea that it was in danger and needed rescuing, he could not tell. But he was sure that Liz had finally come to a decision about what she was going to do.

Afterwards he hung around at the bar for a few minutes, finishing off his drink and listening to Derek make approving noises about Liz's vocals. He had started thinking about the new night shift – already he was looking forward to it. Everything had gone well so far, Clive King, Megan Roach and Duffy having all accepted offers to join the staff. He knew that if Liz had decided to take the job in London, he wouldn't be going with her.

Liz had arranged for him to go backstage after the set so that he could meet Chip and the rest of the group. It was not something he was particularly looking forward to, but he dutifully made his way towards the doorway at the rear of the stage, pushing past the tide of people heading the other way towards the exit. But Liz emerged before he reached the door.

She had changed out of her stage costume and was dressed in her civilian clothes – a loose-fitting white skirt tucked into mustard-coloured cords. She grinned at him, her hair stuck to her forehead with sweat.

'You were good,' he said, meaning it. 'That Old Magic.'

'It was fun. What did you think of the group?'

Charlie hesitated, then said, 'Promising.'

'I know what you mean – they're still a bit rough at the edges. But they've got plenty of energy and ambition.'

'And volume.'

'Chip's determined to be a mega-star before he's twenty-one.'

'Stranger things have happened.'

She brushed her hair back off her face. 'Shall we go home?'

'I thought you wanted me to meet the band?'

'Do you want to?'

'Well – some other time, maybe. Not thinking of signing you up permanently, are they?'

'Oh, no. That was definitely a one-off as far as I'm concerned. Twenty-eight is too old to be stomping the stage every night.'

136

Most of the crowd had already melted away. Charlie and Liz went out through a side-exit into the alleyway where his car was parked. She squeezed his knee as he clipped his seat-belt into place, but said nothing. He drove off.

A light rain began to fall, and he switched on the wipers. The silence in the car was drowned by the sound of them flicking across the windscreen.

'I'm not going to take the job,' Liz said.

Charlie waited, but she did not elaborate.

'Do you want to tell me why?' he asked.

In the periphery of his vision, he saw her shrug. 'Maybe I don't feel I'm ready for it. Maybe I'm not sure I want to move to London. Maybe I'm making a big mistake.'

Charlie overtook a car which had been weaving down the road ahead of them, giving it a wide berth. The driver had probably had one too many. He himself had been drinking shandy all evening; it wasn't exactly his favourite drink, but at least it allowed you to get home safely.

'Listen,' he said, 'I hope you haven't decided against it because . . .'

'It's nothing to do with you,' she interrupted. 'Well, it is, but not in the way you think.'

'What way is that?'

'I didn't turn it down because you wanted to stay here. Just to keep us together.'

'I'm glad that wasn't a factor,' he said sarcastically.

'You know what I mean.'

'No, Liz, I don't.'

She sighed heavily. 'Can we just forget about it for now? I've turned it down, and that's that.'

He did not reply. For a while there was silence, and then Liz said, 'I thought you'd be glad.'

'I am,' he told her. 'I just don't feel that we worked it out properly.'

They had reached their flat and he pulled over, cut the engine. He stared at her, waiting for some response.

'I'm tired, Charlie,' she said. 'Let's go in and go to bed.'

As they climbed the stairs, Charlie could hear the telephone ringing inside the flat. He hurriedly opened the door and went into the living room.

'Charlie Fairhead,' he said into the receiver.

'Charlie, it's Ewart. I'm sorry to ring so late, but something's cropped up. Is it convenient to talk?'

Liz had entered and was staring at him questioningly. He mouthed the word 'Coffee' and she nodded, went into the kitchen.

'Sure,' Charlie said to Ewart. 'What's the problem?'

'It's Clive King. Or rather his father. There's been a big family upset.'

Charlie had a vague memory of Clive mentioning that his father was an invalid, suffering some form of dementia. And now Ewart was telling him that the old man had apparently escaped from the house a week ago and had been missing for three days. Eventually a crane driver at Holby Docks had found him in a lean-to shack next to a warehouse. He had been dead for at least twenty-four hours.

'Apparently he went missing in only his pyjamas,' Ewart said, 'and it was raining heavily on that day. He caught pneumonia, and without medical attention it finished him off in no time at all. It looks as if he'd been hiding out in the shack for the best part of a week, with Clive hunting everywhere for him.'

'That's terrible.'

'Clive sounded as if he was still in a state of shock –

and little wonder. He also sounded exhausted. He rang to say that he doesn't think he'll be able to join us on the new shift. His GP's advised him to take a fortnight's complete rest.'

Liz came in and handed him his coffee.

'We'll have to get a replacement,' Ewart said.

'That's a damn shame. He's a good man.'

'I had the same impression when I met him, but there's nothing we can do.'

'Did he say when the funeral was?'

'Two o'clock, the day after tomorrow. Are you going to go?'

'It's the least I can do. Is he backing out of the shift permanently?'

'He didn't say. I think he needs some time to think it over.'

'That's something, anyway. It's probably best if we don't do anything for the moment. I'll give you a call tomorrow.'

Ewart rang off, and Charlie put the phone down. The bedroom door was open, and Liz was standing just inside in the swathe of light, taking off her bra and panties.

Charlie walked into her, still holding his coffee.

'I need cheering up,' he said, po-faced.

She peered at him, grinned. 'Let's see what I can do.'

She reached forward, and with one swift movement unzipped his jeans.

10

The coffin lay beside the grave on milky plastic sheets. Clive's eyes kept flickering from it to the neatly cut hole in the ground – a deep hole, into which his father's body would descend for ever.

Around the graveside everyone's heads were bowed as Ray Hurley recited a prayer. Clive couldn't concentrate on it, couldn't keep his eyes off the coffin. Although he could not see his father, he wanted to absorb every last memory of him, even encased in wood, before the earth swallowed him up.

The funeral was well attended, with perhaps a hundred people or more standing in the grassy cemetery amongst the ranks of tombstones which stretched in all directions, all that remained of hundreds of lives.

Lord, he prayed, give me strength.

He had become so familiar with death in the course of his work, and yet only now did he seem to have discovered real grief. He had been close to his mother, had been sad when she'd passed away – but this was far more devastating somehow. If only I could have seen him alive once more, he thought, I could have . . .

Could have what? Apologized? Explained? Pleaded with him? But all of these would have been useless since his father had long gone beyond reason and ordinary emotion. There was nothing he could have said or done that would have made any difference. And yet he still wished that he had had the chance.

The Reverend Hurley was now talking, and Clive did

his best to look attentive. His wife and two sons stood beside him, and behind them were other family members, some of whom had travelled from London, Liverpool and even Newcastle to attend the funeral. And there were old friends of the family whom he hadn't seen in decades. His father had always been popular. Lovable, they called him, like a big black bear.

He blinked the wetness from his eyes. Some of the women were sobbing and moaning behind him, but it was all restrained and dignified, as his father would have wanted it. Despite his jokes and laughter, he'd always been a sober man in his habits. Devout, too.

Clive had no doubt that his father's soul would be welcomed in Heaven, and this thought was an uplifting one. He wasn't sad for his father, he realized, but for himself. Sad and bitter.

Bitter?

Yes, he could no longer deny it. A part of him still resented the fact that his father had treated him so badly in his last years, even though he knew that the old man couldn't help himself. It had made those last few years a constant torment for him. Secretly he had wanted to shout at him, to rage at him for being unfair, for constantly rejecting his love and concern.

Only now could he admit this to himself. And having done so, he could feel his anger slowly beginning to evaporate.

The coffin was now being lowered into the grave. Still he could not concentrate on what Ray Hurley was saying. He was aware of a line of trees in the background, of white clouds uncoiling gently across the sky, of darkness and shade crossing the cemetery as they hid then revealed the sun. But the words were just a drone.

He glanced at Leah, then at Errol and Bobby. The two

boys were frowning, as though vaguely puzzled by the whole proceedings, while Leah caught his eye and gave a small smile. She reached up and squeezed his arm. It was all that was needed.

He had managed to track down a few dockers who'd seen his father wandering around the wharves in the two days before he had died. They hadn't suspected that he was ill and had thought that he was just another crazy tramp – he had found an old overcoat which had hidden his pyjamas. He'd been babbling about wanting to get a ship to Jamaica. He wanted to go home, to die there. In the shack where they had found him dead, there'd been a tattered colour brochure, advertising holidays in the Caribbean.

Clive became aware that he was now required to lead the procession past the grave. He stepped forward, knelt, and scooped up a handful of brown earth. It was still moist from the rain. The coffin seemed to be lying a long way down, the clayey sides of the rectangle surrounding it cut perfectly. As he tossed his handful of earth down on to the wood, he had his final realization: he was *relieved* that his father was finally dead.

Ray Hurley was holding his arms and whispering condolences. Clive smiled at him, nodded, moved on. He felt as if the last of his paralysing grief was dropping off him, leaving a normal sorrow and pain. He knew now that he would be able to go through the normal process of bereavement rather than having his father's death gnawing at him like a wound that wouldn't heal.

Relief. Relief that both his father's torment had ended, and his own. Ever since he and Leah had taken him into their home to look after him, he'd felt like an intruder there, having to avoid his father as much as possible or risk encounters in which his suspicion and hostility was

142

relentless. Now it was all over, and he could concentrate on the memory of his father as the warm and loving man he had been before his illness had changed him.

The line of cars which had brought them to the funeral was standing on the road nearby. Clive led Leah and the boys towards the leading car.

'Dad,' said Bobby, 'are we going to have football practice today?'

'No,' Clive said. 'Not today.'

'When then?'

'We'll see. Soon.'

In a way he was glad that neither of the boys had really grasped what their grandfather's death meant. They were far too young for grief, and they would have their share of unhappiness as they grew older – it was everyone's fate. Far better that they focused on the football. Although he had not been able to attend the game, his team had won their semi-final, and would be playing the talented Eastmead School for the cup in a week's time. Clive felt a renewed determination to ensure that they were well trained in the days leading up to the game. The boys would be thrilled if they actually managed to carry off the trophy.

As the family approached their car, Clive saw two men standing nearby. They had obviously attended the funeral service, but had remained some distance away so that they wouldn't intrude. Clive now recognized them as Charlie Fairhead and Ewart Plimmer.

Charlie had been a friend of his for some years, and Clive appreciated his appearance at the burial. But Ewart Plimmer hardly knew him, and his attendance was tremendously gratifying. Clive felt an even greater respect for the man.

'Wait here for a moment,' he said to the boys. Then he walked over to where Charlie and Ewart were standing.

'Thank you for coming,' he said to the two of them. 'It's good of you.'

'How are Errol and Bobby taking it?' Charlie asked.

'In their stride,' Clive told him. He smiled.

'If there's anything we can do,' Ewart began.

'No, but thank you. I've just realized that I'm relieved it's finally over.'

Ewart nodded understandingly. 'Sometimes it's for the best, even though that sounds like a cliché.'

'It was much harder with him being alive but not in his right mind.'

'You still on leave-of-absence?' Charlie asked.

Clive nodded.

'Make the most of it. Rest up, and relax.'

'Actually I feel ready to get back to work. I was wondering. About the new night shift.'

'Yes?' said Ewart.

'Well, if you haven't got a replacement for me yet, then I'd like to give it a go from Day One.'

11

Ewart was eating a lunch of baked beans on toast when he heard Ros's car pull up outside the house. He had managed to burn both the beans and the toast, and the resulting mess was enough to dull anyone's appetite. He scraped the meal into the flip-top bin beside the cooker as he heard Ros's key turn in the front-door lock.

She had stayed at Madge's for a further week, and had only phoned him that morning to say that she was coming back. Today was D-day, with the night shift starting at seven that evening, and Ewart was convinced that Ros had delayed her return to cause him the maximum amount of inconvenience.

He put his plate and cutlery in the sink and stood there, feeling like a schoolboy awaiting the arrival of the headmistress. Ros entered, dressed in a new apricot mohair sweater over a chocolate brown skirt.

'You look nice,' he said, coming forward to kiss her.

She turned her head slightly so that his kiss landed on her cheek rather than her lips. Immediately he saw that she was staring at the burnt pan on the cooker.

'How's Madge?' he said.

'She's fine. A lot better.'

'We had a postcard from Sarah. She's in the Dordogne.'

He had left the card on the work unit beside the fridge. Ros picked it up, read it through quickly, then put it down again. She peered out through the kitchen window.

'The garden looks nice,' she said sarcastically. He

145

had done nothing with it, and weeds still grew thickly everywhere.

'I'm sorry,' he said. 'Somehow I just never managed to find the time . . .'

'No. I didn't think you would.'

'Ros . . .'

'Yes?' She turned to face him once more.

'I think we have to talk.'

'Not now, Ewart. I'm not in the mood.'

'When then? We can't go on like this, can we?'

'It'll have to wait until I get back.'

'Get back? From where?'

'New Zealand. Madge and I are going to stay with Gerald for a few weeks. We're leaving first thing in the morning. I only called in to pack a suitcase.'

Ewart stared at her. She looked determined, but she was avoiding his eye.

'When was all this arranged?' he asked.

'A few days ago.'

'You might have told me about it before now.'

'Like you told me about this new job of yours?'

'That isn't the same thing.'

'Isn't it? It seems to me that we haven't got much to say to one another these days about anything.'

'That's because you haven't been here.'

'I needed a break, Ewart. We both needed a break from one another. I also need a holiday. And since it was obvious to me that you weren't interested, I decided to organize one for me and Madge. I've been wanting to see Gerald and his family, and the trip will do Madge good.'

'So it's all settled, is it?'

'Yes. Though there'd probably be time for you to book a seat on the plane with us if you wanted to.'

'You know I can't. Not now.'

146

She nodded in a way that indicated that she had anticipated his reply. Ewart was beginning to feel very angry, but he did his best to keep his temper under control.

'How long are you going to be away?' he asked.

'As I said, a few weeks. Not more than a month, I expect. It depends on how long Gerald can put us up.'

Ewart knew that he had a big house and would let them stay for as long as they wished.

'If you'd let me know in advance,' he said, 'then perhaps I would have been able to make arrangements so that I could come with you.'

'Well, it's done now.'

'You didn't want me to come, did you? You just wanted to arrange it so that I'll feel guilty about not being able to.'

'Think what you want to,' she said, walking past him into the hallway. 'I'm not going to argue about it now.'

He stood in the doorway, watching her climb the stairs.

'We've got to talk,' he insisted.

'There's no time now. We'll talk when I get back.'

He followed her up the stairs. She went into the bedroom and dragged out the suitcase from under the bed.

'Is this a separation, Ros?'

'You can call it what you like. For me, it's going to be the holiday I've needed.'

'And afterwards?'

She had gone to the wardrobe and was taking out dresses and skirts and blouses. Only now did she look at him directly. 'Afterwards we're going to have to decide whether we can save our marriage.'

* * *

'Is it that bad?' Charlie asked Liz across the candlelit table. She was prodding the chili con carne on her plate with her fork.

'It's fine,' she said.

'I know I'm not the world's greatest cook . . .'

'No, really.'

It had taken him most of the afternoon to prepare the meal, and he had worked hard to get it just right, not rushing anything. The previous evening he'd suggested to Liz that she come home early from work the following day so that they could have a cosy dinner before he went off on his first night's work with the new Casualty unit. He'd had to draw the curtains on the still-bright evening in order to make the candlelight effective, and he'd bought a single red rose and put it in a glass at the centre of the white tablecloth.

Normally he was not the romantic type prone to such gestures, but he'd felt that some effort was needed. Ever since Liz had told him that she'd turned down the job with City Sounds, things had been rather strained between them, with long silences punctuated by awkward snatches of conversation. Their love-making was clumsy and self-conscious, as though they were doing it out of duty rather than passion. And yet Liz continued to insist that nothing was wrong. He'd tried to press her, to get to the root of the problem – a problem he was sure lay with her rather than him. It was the job, he suspected; she regretted not taking it. But whenever he suggested this, she denied it strongly.

And the dinner hadn't worked – that much was obvious. Liz looked distracted, lost in her own thoughts. She was scarcely eating, and the wine he had poured for her lay untouched in the glass.

148

Suddenly Charlie had had enough. He'd been uncharacteristically patient and reasonable in recent weeks, but he'd reached the end of his tether. He could feel a slow fury of resentment building within him. Picking up the napkin on his lap, he tossed it on the table.

'I'm sick of this.'

Liz glanced up from her plate. 'What?'

'I said I'm sick of this.'

She tried to make light of it: 'It doesn't taste *that* bad.'

'I'm not talking about the food, as you damn well know. What the hell's going on, Liz?'

'What do you mean?'

'All right, I'll spell it out – for days now you've been moody, miserable, uncommunicative, a right pain in the neck.'

'I'm sorry.'

'It's not apologies I'm after, but reasons. Just what the hell is going on?'

'OK, have it your way.' He pushed his chair back and stood up. 'I'm going out.'

'No, Charlie. Wait.'

She was still looking down at the food on her plate, and now she picked up her napkin and wiped her lips. In a voice muffled by it, she said, 'I slept with him.'

'What?'

She took the napkin away from her mouth. 'Gavin Brownlow. I did sleep with him.'

Charlie did not move or say anything.

'It was only once. But it happened.'

The rose in the glass was tilted towards her. It looked a bit limp.

'I don't believe you,' he said.

'It's the truth, Charlie.'

She was hunched in her chair as though expecting to be

slapped, the napkin twisted in her hands. The flickering candlelight made shadows move across her face.

'Why?' said Charlie. 'Because you thought it would get you the job?'

'No. I just fancied him.'

'You bitch.'

'I didn't plan it. It just happened.'

'Accident, was it?'

'It only happened once.'

'So you said.'

'It was a couple of days after he arrived – '

'Christ, I don't want to know the details!'

'I'm only trying to explain. We were both pretty drunk, and we kind of fell into it. It was pretty awful, and afterwards I told him I wasn't interested again. He accepted that.'

'Still, you managed to get a few more free meals out of him, didn't you?'

'That's unfair.'

'Is it? Is it, Liz? I think there's unfairer things than that. Like you playing me for a Number One Sucker.'

'It wasn't like that.'

'Oh? What was it like then? Did the earth move for you?'

She said nothing to this. Charlie wanted to throw things at her, to wound her badly with words. But at the same time he felt that it was all futile.

'That's why I didn't take the job,' Liz said. 'Because I would have felt that I'd got it on false pretences.'

'Very bloody noble of you.'

'You've got every right to be angry because I didn't tell you right away.'

'Oh, I see. It's all right to fool around with other people, is it, so long as you own up immediately after.'

'We're not married, Charlie. You never wanted to be.'

'I never heard you pleading with me to tie the knot. We've been as good as married these last few years, and what's the point of living together as a couple if you're going to leap into bed with anyone you fancy?'

'I don't make a habit of it, Charlie. It hasn't happened before.'

'I've only got your word for that. Maybe you've got a few more revelations up your sleeve.'

'Look, I've been unhappy because I haven't been able to tell you about it.'

'That's very gratifying. Well, you've eased your conscience now, haven't you?'

Charlie snatched his jacket off the back of the door.

'Where are you going?' Liz asked.

'I'm going where I can be bloody useful to people, not just a mug. And as far as I'm concerned, you can go to hell!'

Ewart had decided to set out early for the hospital. Ros had packed her bags and left as swiftly as possible, and the house seemed filled with the void of her abrupt departure. He wanted to be busy, to be occupied with his work so that he could ignore the uncertainties of his personal life.

He locked the front door behind him and headed down the path. His car was parked outside the gate. But as he was about to get into it, he happened to glance towards Joyce's house. Immediately he stopped.

On top of the low brick wall in front of the house were several rose bushes. They were still in their wrapping, and they looked as if they had been dumped there.

Ewart walked over to the house. Joyce had always kept an immaculate front garden – competition between

151

her and Ros had always been fierce if discreet – but the lawn had deep gouges all over it, the turf peeled back to reveal the dark earth below. Clumps of flowers had also been torn from their beds and lay scattered everywhere.

Ewart pushed open the gate and walked up the path. The front door hung open.

'Joyce?' he said, stepping to the hall. 'Joyce?'

There was no reply.

A potted plant had been overturned at the bottom of the stairs, and broken china and earth had been trodden into the dove-grey carpet. With a deep sense of foreboding, Ewart pushed open the door to the living room.

Magazines lay scattered over the sofa and the floor, and the coffee table had been overturned, its smoked glass centre shattered. Drawers had been opened, napkins, table mats and cutlery spilling from them.

Ewart moved into the kitchen. There was broken crockery over the floor, covered with a dusting of soap powder. Coffee had been splashed over the walls, a loaf of sliced bread had been dumped in the sink, a pan was sitting on the still-burning gas ring of the cooker.

Ewart switched the ring off. At first he had suspected burglary, but now he revised his opinion. Hurrying back out into the hallway, he called up the stairs, 'Joyce? Are you there? It's Ewart Plimmer.'

Silence.

He climbed the stairs. The bathroom door was ajar at the top, and two towels lay damp and twisted on the floor. But there was no one inside.

He moved across the landing towards the bedroom.

This, too, was a mess. Clothes had been pulled from the two wardrobes, and were draped all over the floor. On the dressing table a clutter of perfume bottles and cosmetics had been overturned, and lipstick was scrawled over the mirror. It took Ewart a moment to realize that the scrawl was, in fact, writing. In linked script it read *To hell with it!*

Ewart moved further into the room. The duvet and pillows on the bed had been piled into a heap at its centre. And lying on the floor between the bed and the window was Joyce.

She was not dead, or even unconscious. Wrapped in a black fur coat, she lay on one arm, gazing towards the window. On the floor beside her was a bottle of Gordon's, and she had a glass in her hand.

'Joyce?' he said, moving slowly towards her.

'What do you want?' she said without looking at him.

He crouched beside her. She was wearing nothing under the coat.

'What's been happening?' he said softly.

She did not move or speak.

'Joyce . . .?'

'Is this a professional or private call?'

Though he was practically certain she hadn't been burgled, he said, 'Did someone break in?'

'I did it.'

She took a gulp of her drink, half of it trickling down the side of her face. Two thirds of the gin bottle was empty, he saw, and there was a brown bottle of tablets on the beside cabinet over her head.

'A dream home, Donald called it when we moved in here.' She gave a sour laugh. 'Like a bloody prison, as far as I'm concerned. All I do is clean and tidy the place, day in, day out. It's bloody ridiculous – Donald's never here to appreciate it. There's only me.'

She hiccuped, swallowed another mouthful of gin. Ewart could see that she was very drunk, but he was also worried about the tablets. Reaching up surreptitiously, he grabbed the bottle. It still had its top on, but there was nothing inside. The label read PROTHIADEN 75 mg.

'I haven't taken any, if that's what you're thinking.'

She had looked around and seen him taking the bottle.

'These were prescribed by your GP?' he asked.

'By my psychiatrist.'

She was sitting up now, the coat wrapped tight around her, the drink still in her hand.

'Yes,' she said, 'you didn't know, did you? I've been seeing one for months. Dr Mowbray. Know her?'

'Yes. She's good.'

'She states the obvious, if you ask me. After half a dozen sessions she told me that I was suffering from loneliness and depression.' She gave a dismissive laugh. 'I could have told her that at the start.'

Her eyes had a drugged look to them, but there was no way of telling whether this was due to the alcohol she had drunk or whether she had swallowed the tablets in the bottle. But the date of prescription was a month ago, and assuming she had been following the recommended dosage of one tablet a day, the bottle would have been used up by now.

'Donald has a mistress, you know,' Joyce said. 'His secretary. It's so predictable and sordid.' She drained the rest of the gin in her glass, then poured out some more.

'Don't you think you've had enough of that?' Ewart said.

'Concerned, are you? Worried that I might do something foolish?'

'Of course I am.'

'Donald bought me this coat,' she said, indicating the fur. 'It doesn't even fit properly. I hate him. That's why I

154

made a mess around the house – because it's his place. I was so tired of keeping all my anger in. Do you think I'm attractive?'

Ewart was taken aback by this question, but he did his best not to show it.

'Yes,' he said honestly. 'I do. But – '

'Don't worry, I'm not going to try to get you into bed with me. I've met Donald's secretary, you know – the one he's having an affair with. She's not half as good-looking as me. That's what I can't understand.'

Suddenly she began to cry. The tears came convulsively, rolling down her cheeks. Ewart took the glass out of her hand, lifted her gently up and simply held her as she sobbed against his shoulder. Another casualty, he thought sadly; right here on my back door.

Gradually the tears subsided. Then she pulled away from him and said, 'I feel sick.'

He helped her across the landing and into the bathroom. She made for the toilet bowl, but he forced her across to the bath, his doctor's instincts now at the fore. He wanted to be sure that she hadn't swallowed a handful of tablets, and the contents of her stomach would give him a clue.

For five minutes he held her as she retched and retched. At last it was over. He could see nothing to indicate that she had taken an overdose.

'How do you feel?' he asked.

'On top of the world,' she said sarcastically.

He dampened a flannel to clean her face, but she insisted on doing it herself. Her eyes were bloodshot, but there did not appear to be any abnormal dilation of the pupils.

Suddenly she shivered and said, 'I'm cold.'

At this point Ewart heard a woman's voice on the stairway: 'Joyce? Joyce?'

'It's Dr Mowbray,' Joyce informed him. 'I phoned her an hour ago.'

12

'So you're on this new shift, eh?' John Naughton said to Lawrence Clarke.

Lawrence nodded, his mouth full of sausage and fried egg.

'Wouldn't fancy Casualty myself,' Naughton said. 'Not twelve hours a night, anyway.'

Lawrence shrugged, stabbing some chips with his fork. 'I'm going to give it a try. We have to serve our time some way, don't we?'

Both men were newly qualified doctors, and so were required to spend some time in hospital work before they specialized.

'Sounds a bit too hectic to me,' Naughton said, attacking a sticky bun. 'Ewart Plimmer's in charge, isn't he?'

'That's right.'

'I trained with him for a while. Knows his stuff, but he's a bit – well, *zealous*, if you know what I mean. Works you hard, total commitment to the NHS, and all that. Anyone would swear we were being paid a king's ransom for our services.'

'I know what you mean. He wants the staff gathered for a briefing an hour before we open shop.'

Naughton glanced at the clock on the wall of Max's café. 'You're going to be late.'

Lawrence swallowed a mouthful of mushrooms. 'Can't see the point in it myself. These sort of things are just pep talks for the more junior staff. Plimmer believes in

157

all that psychology stuff – with the patients, too. He's a bit old fashioned if you ask me.'

Naughton nodded sagely. 'Know what you mean. Medicine's a matter of science and technology now, and penicillin's done far more good for people than any amount of Freudian mumbo-jumbo. We're doctors, for God's sake, not bloody social workers.'

A man in his early twenties with long greasy blond hair came up to the table. He wore a grubby white apron, and he was holding out a plate of fried food.

'You order this?' he asked Naughton in a nasal voice.

'Certainly not,' Naughton said.

The man sniffed, then wandered away like a sleepwalker.

'Who the devil was that?' Naughton asked.

'His name's Clyde,' Lawrence told him.

'Where's Max?'

'Wife had her op today, apparently, and he's visiting. Clyde's standing in. He's a friend of the cook.'

Naughton stared after him. 'He looks bloody incompetent to me. Just like the bloody cook – what's his name?'

'Morton,' Lawrence said, dabbing some egg yolk from his chin with a serviette.

'I had an omelette in here the other day, and it was disgusting. I'm sure he used powdered egg. And that stuff you're eating looks revolting.'

'It fills you up,' Lawrence said, pushing another forkful of sausage into his mouth. 'I can never go to work on an empty stomach. Especially on nights.'

Ewart was just winding up the briefing when the door to the staff room opened. In walked Lawrence Clarke.

158

'Ah,' said Ewart, 'come in, Doctor Clarke. I'm glad you could join us.'

Ewart saw the hint of a scowl on Clarke's face as all eyes in the room turned to him.

'Sorry I'm late,' Lawrence said, sitting down on a chair beside the door. 'Car trouble.'

'I was just explaining to everyone that this unit is on trial,' Ewart said. 'We have a year in which to prove ourselves, and if we don't, the entire Casualty Department here could well be closed down.'

'I thought the idea was to centralize facilities,' Lawrence said.

'That's just a bureaucratic euphemism,' Charlie interrupted. 'What it means in practice is that there'd be fewer medical facilities for people in the city.'

'I tend to agree with Mr Fairhead,' Ewart said, 'and so it's important that this unit does well – justifies its existence. As the Clinical Assistant I'll be taking a background role in the actual treatment side of the unit, but I want you all to know that I will be available for advice or consultation whenever you feel you might need it. I'm not just saying that as a formality – I mean it. If you have any problems beyond the immediate demands of treating patients, then you can always come to me.'

Ewart has finished. Charlie rose.

'OK,' he said to his staff, 'let's get on with it.'

By seven-thirty, the waiting area was already half-full with a random assortment of minor injuries – cuts, burns, a possible fracture, and a six-year-old child with something in his eye. The unit's receptionist, Susie Shastri, watched the child from her desk as his mother tried to keep him occupied. The boy was perched on her knee, and she was reading a book to him. But he kept trying to

159

rub his eye, and cried when she stopped him from doing so.

'Won't be long,' she told him. 'Won't be long.'

Charlie Fairhead walked up to the desk and said, 'Have you seen Doctor Clarke, Susie?'

'I think he just went into the toilet,' she told him.

'Again? That's the third time in the last half hour.'

'Said he was feeling a bit queasy.'

Charlie stared down the corridor where the toilets were, then murmured, 'Hasn't got the stomach for a bit of hard work, if you ask me.'

'Oh, dear. It sounds like there's going to be friction in the ranks.'

'It's purely personal. Who's next?'

'Thomas Atkinson,' she said, handing him a card on which the details of the patient's complaint were written. 'He's the young boy over there with his mum.'

Charlie took the card from her and walked over to them.

'Hello, tiger,' he said to the boy. 'What's the trouble?'

'I got a thing in my eye,' the boy told him.

'So have I,' Charlie said. 'It's my eyeball.'

The boy screwed up his nose at this awful joke. Charlie gently scooped the boy up into his arms, glancing at the mother as he did so and winking at her. She smiled back at him and said, 'He won't let me touch it. I think it's a bit of gravel.'

The boy's eye was inflamed and weeping. Charlie made funny faces at him as he peered at it.

'You're silly,' the boy said.

'That's what my mum's always telling me,' Charlie replied. 'Well, then, shall we go and get that thing out of your eye?'

He began to lead the boy off towards one of the cubicles, the mother following.

'Will it hurt?' the boy asked.

'Not if you don't squiggle.'

'What's "squiggle" mean?'

'It's a cross between "squirm" and "wriggle". Know what twichet means?'

Their voices diminished until they were lost in the background murmur of the unit. Susie took a mirror from her bag and studied her reflection, checking that her make-up was in order. She was an attractive twenty-four-year-old, with brown eyes, black shoulder-length hair and a brilliant white smile which could lighten up her whole face. Her parents had come to England from India in 1952; she and her two younger brothers had all been born in Holby. She enjoyed her work and had taken the job with the night-shift to escape the perpetual arguments with her parents, who were always complaining that she was too Westernized, with no respect for her native culture. But to her, British born and bred, England was her native land, with more opportunities for women to be independent and make a career for themselves. She nurtured the secret ambition of becoming a fashion model, and had done photographic sessions for calendars and a mail-order catalogue. Working nights at the hospital meant that her afternoons could be kept free in case other work of this sort came her way.

Ewart and Duffy appeared, having just checked the store cupboards to ensure that they had all the equipment they needed. They stopped near Susie's desk.

'We're filling up with patients,' Ewart said to Duffy. 'Charlie will probably need you now.'

Duffy departed. Ewart lingered at Susie's desk.

'An interesting girl,' he told Susie with reference to

Duffy. 'She told me a fortune-teller predicted that she was going to meet me.'

'My parents are superstitious,' Susie replied. 'I think it's a load of old cobblers.'

'Oh, I wouldn't go that far. "There are more things in heaven and earth than are dreamt of in our philosophy."'

'Is that a quote?'

'Shakespeare. *King Lear*, I think. A bit rusty on the bard.' Ewart glanced around the waiting area. 'Everything all right?'

'So far. No drunks yet.'

'It's early.'

'I know. I'm keeping my fingers crossed.'

Ewart departed. A few seconds later, Lawrence Clarke emerged from the men's toilet. Susie thought he looked a little pale as he approached her desk.

'Are you all right?' she asked him.

'I'm fine,' he said in a clipped voice. 'Why do you ask?'

'I just thought – you look a bit pale.'

'A touch of indigestion, that's all. What have you got for me?'

She passed him a card and indicated a man in his forties who was sitting quietly at the end of the row, a hand-towel wrapped around his right hand.

'What's this?' Lawrence said, reading the card. 'Cut his hand on a bread knife? Sounds pretty trifling to me – why can't he see his GP in the morning instead of bothering us here?'

'I think it's pretty bad,' Susie said. The towel the man was holding was white, but it was already soaked through with blood.

Lawrence, however, hadn't noticed this. He gave a weary sigh.

'Oh well,' he said, 'I suppose I'd better see him. Mustn't forget we're public servants, must we?'

With poor grace, he went over to the man and said, 'Mr Knapp? Please follow me.'

No other patients had come in during the last ten minutes. Susie flicked through the pages of a copy of *Cosmopolitan*, studying the way models posed in glossy photographs, making a note of what they were wearing.

'I am here to introduce myself formally,' said a voice.

Susie looked up. A man in his forties with dark hair and a moustache was standing there, holding out his hand. Susie had seen him earlier at the briefing, but they had not actually spoken; he was the porter on the night shift.

'I am Stanislaw Dabrowska,' he said. 'You can call me Stan.'

His hand was reaching out over the desk. Susie took it and shook.

'Pleased to meet you,' she said.

'And I you, too. We will get along fine, yes?'

'I certainly hope so.'

'Tell me – do you know how many times a hair can be split?'

'Pardon?' He spoke English with a Polish accent, and Susie was not sure that she had heard him correctly.

Stan plucked a hair from his head with not even a wince. He held it out. 'A human hair. Very thin, you would agree?'

'Well,' said Susie, 'yes.'

'So how many times do you think it can be split?'

'You mean lengthways?'

'Of course. If it is split sideways, then it is not split but cut, yes?'

'I suppose so.'

'So how many times can it be split?'

163

'Has someone tried it?' Susie asked, noticing a fat paperback tucked under his arm. It was entitled *Facts To Amaze*.

'Certainly they have. An Englishman holds the record. He was once a champion cyclist.'

'Oh,' said Susie, feeling as if she was losing the already tenuous thread of the conversation. 'Does being a good cyclist help you split hairs?'

'Of course not. That is a coincidence. But you have still not answered my question – how many times?'

'Six?' Susie offered.

'Wrong,' said Stan with a smile. 'Try again.'

'Ten?'

'Seventeen!' he told her triumphantly. 'This man has split a human hair seventeen times on several occasions. Is that not a remarkable fact?'

'Amazing,' Susie had to agree. 'But tell me something – why did he do it?'

'Why?' Stan looked astounded that the question had been asked, but also slightly puzzled. 'For the world record, of course.'

'In hair splitting?'

'Indeed. Do you know the word "Squassation"?'

'What?'

'"Squassation". What does this word mean?'

'It sounds like a revolting disease.'

'No, no,' said Stan, beaming. 'It is a system of punishment, of torture. A man has his hands tied together and his feet weighted down with stones or irons. Then he is jerked up and down by a rope. This is squassation.'

Susie didn't quite know what to say. Stan seemed pleasant enough, but a bit eccentric.

'Another one,' Stan continued. 'Who said, "A foolish consistency is the hobgoblin of little minds"?'

'Uh,' said Susie, 'that's a quote, right?'

'It is.'

'That's the second I've heard in the last fifteen minutes.'

'The second what?'

'Quote. The last was from Shakespeare.'

'Ah,' said Stan. 'What was it?'

'Something about there being more things under heaven and earth – '

'"There are more things in heaven and earth, Horatio, than are dreamt of in your philosophy".'

'Yeah. That sounds about right.'

'*Hamlet*, Act One, Scene Five.'

'Is that a fact?'

Stan tapped the side of his head. 'I store everything here. Facts. I study books, and I remember. Dates, times, names, places. Medical facts, too. Always I am studying. One day, when I have learnt enough, I will write in to *Mastermind* and ask Magnus Magnusson for a seat in the hot chair.'

'Oh,' said Susie. 'I get it. You're in training for quizzes.'

Stan nodded enthusiastically. 'I hope to go on other shows, too, and win cocktail cabinets, hi-fi equipment, holidays in Greece. Perhaps a cuddly toy, too, yes?'

Susie smiled at his little joke. A patient approached the desk, and Stan made to move away.

'We will talk again,' he said as he departed. 'Before I go, I will tell you who said "A foolish consistency is the hobgoblin of little minds". It was Emerson.'

He wandered off down the corridor towards his lodge. Susie's boyfriend had recently been playing her some old rock albums from the 'sixties and 'seventies; she wondered – could this possibly be the Emerson of Emerson, Lake and Palmer?

* * *

The telephone in Ewart's office rang.

'Ewart Plimmer, Casualty Department.'

'Ewart, it's Jeannett Mowbray here. You asked me to ring you about Joyce Simmonds, the neighbour of yours.'

'Ah, yes. How is she?'

Ewart and Dr Mowbray had managed to persuade Joyce to go to the hospital, just to check that she hadn't swallowed anything toxic. Dr Mowbray had driven her there, leaving Ewart to clear up the worst of the mess in the house before he hurried off to brief the night-shift. He felt a little guilty that he hadn't had time to enquire after her welfare.

'She's all right,' Jeanette Mowbray told him. 'She's depressed, but she's still functioning.'

'No overdose?'

'No. Blood and gastric juices were clean. She'd just over-indulged on the gin. We kept her under observation for a couple of hours, but then she insisted on going home.'

'You discharged her?'

'She became panicky because she'd run out of antide-pressants. I gave her a couple of tablets to tide her over until tomorrow. I'm seeing her at ten-thirty in the morning.'

'But the house . . .'

'She wanted to get back to tidy it up. She's over the worst, Ewart, believe me. A large part of her problem is her inability to express anger, and it's probably done her the world of good.'

'I would have thought that her problem is her husband.'

'Well, yes, that's the practical side of it, as it were. But there's not much we can do about that, is there? We can only try to make her psychologically strong enough so that she can do something about it herself.'

166

This was all too depressingly true. Too often, medicine could only treat the symptoms of sickness, be it physical or mental, while the circumstances which had created the original problem were beyond its control.

He thanked Dr Mowbray for ringing, and hung up. He had met her at a medical conference several years back, and she had a good reputation as a psychiatrist, eschewing psychological dogma where it conflicted with her patients' needs. But Joyce had seemed so distressed . . .

He found her home number in his telephone book, and dialled it. The phone rang for some time, then suddenly he heard Joyce's voice said, 'Hello?'

'Joyce, it's Ewart Plimmer. I was just calling to find out how you were feeling.'

'Much better now, thank you. I'm sorry about what happened.'

'I'm just glad I happened to be passing. Are you sure you're all right?'

'I'm a bit tired, but that's only to be expected. Nora Baker's with me. She's been helping me clear up.'

'Ah,' said Ewart. 'That's good.' Nora Baker was a widow who lived nearby – a warm-hearted, no-nonsense type who would be the ideal sort of company for Joyce in the circumstances.

'She's staying with me tonight. I'll be fine.'

'If you need anything . . .'

'It was kind of you to help. I only wish Donald was half the man you are.'

13

She liked being out best after darkness had fallen, when she could wander as she pleased without having people staring at her all the time. If she wanted to talk to herself, that was her business; if she wanted to have a few drinks, that was nothing to do with them.

She'd had a tin of Kit-e-Kat for her tea, eaten straight from the can. She liked the taste of it, and it was cheaper than most tinned meat. Then a cup of tea, with a teabag so old she had to wait ages before the water turned a bit brown. No milk; she'd run out. But she'd found a few Ritz in someone's dustbin that morning. Not as nice as a digestive, especially a chocolate-coated one, but they were better than drinking tea without anything.

All through the winter and spring she'd been living in the house. It was better than the road or a park bench, and you didn't get moved along. She'd told none of the others who were on the road about it, and God would punish her for that. But they would have all moved in and then she would have been forced out. In any case, the council were bound to come in the end and start renovating the place. It was lucky that it stood at the end of the road, surrounded by a tangle of privet and elder, with a back garden gate that gave out on the woodland beside the canal. People on the estate couldn't see her coming and going, so no one knew she was living there.

Lucky the electricity and water had been left on, and luckier still that she'd found an old electric kettle that was still working. On the council dump, she'd found it.

So she could make tea for herself whenever she had a teabag, or heat up a tin of spaghetti when she had a few coppers to spare for food. There was an old mattress upstairs and a cushion off an old settee for a pillow. She piled the overcoats she'd collected on top of her at nights when the weather was really cold.

Most days she had dinner at the Salvation Army, where they didn't ask you too many questions. That was enough to keep her going for the rest of the day, so then she usually went begging, asking for money for food, though it was really for drink. That was a sin, too, and she had become shameless about it. But then she had committed so many sins there was no point in thinking that God would ever forgive her.

She rinsed her cup out, making sure that all the water went into the plastic bowl rather than straight down the sink; she didn't want any neighbours hearing the sound of running water from the house. She'd tip the bowl on the garden when she got back later, after everyone was asleep.

Yesterday it had been cold, but she'd found a belt which she now tied around her overcoat. A thin silver-painted belt, probably from a young woman's outfit. She was old and haggard now, but once she'd been young and had liked pretty clothes. Once she'd been a nurse, looking after people, but that was long ago, before . . .

She didn't want to think about it. Delving into her pocket, she produced a small green bottle of gin. Gordon's. The best. She took a hefty swig. Through the crack in the tin sheeting over the window, she could see that dusk had fallen. It was time to go out.

Normally she went out in the afternoons and didn't come back till long after dark. But today she'd been late at the Salvation Army and hadn't got enough to eat, so she'd sneaked back to the house for tea. She was always careful to check that no one was watching her, especially people peering from windows in the houses nearby. Nosy parkers, who wouldn't hesitate to tell the police or the social services that she was living in the house. All she wanted was to be left alone, so that she could live her life as she pleased. People messed you up, and it was better to have nothing to do with them.

She knew this wasn't a Christian attitude, but she had fallen from grace years ago and was now sunk in sin. Hell-fire awaited her when she died, the flames of eternal damnation. She took another gulp of gin. It helped blunt her thoughts, stopped her thinking about the girl who'd slashed her wrists with a broken Lucozade bottle and lay quietly bleeding to death in her private room while she was busy flirting with a doctor. No one could ever forgive her for that.

The tin sheeting over the kitchen window was loose, and she peered out through the crack, checking that no one was around. Her eyes were still good, and she saw well in the darkness. There were no lights in the house, and even in the middle of the day it was gloomy inside. Sometimes she lit a candle so that she could see what she was doing, but she had to be careful that no one outside noticed the light.

She'd first got into the house through the kitchen window, squeezing her way through on a snowy night when she was desperate to get out of the cold. Then, from the inside, she had been able to push out the sheeting that had been nailed over the back door so that she could come and go that way. Whether coming or going, she always replaced the sheeting after her so the doorway looked undisturbed. That way no one had discovered that she was living in the house.

Time to go. She took a final swig of gin, stuffed the bottle into her overcoat pocket, and gently opened the back door.

A light drizzle was falling as she approached the embankment near the railway station. It was a tall brick wall with a series of arches along its length that housed bricked-up warehouses. This was where everyone gathered after a day on the road. Underneath the arches.

A fire had been lit, she saw, and a dozen men and women were clustered around it, warming their hands. She knew them all – Starchy Harris, Mickey Dunn, Old Rosie – all of them.

'Evening, Else,' Mickey said to her, grinning over the flames. 'Got any booze?'

Else wasn't her real name, but she didn't want anybody to know that. She took her gin bottle from her pocket. It was empty, the cap gone. She turned it upside down before throwing it away. But even so, Mickey scrambled from the fire and picked it up, putting it to his mouth. He sucked and snorted, trying to extract the last drop from the bottle.

'That man has no manners, if you ask me.'

This was Mr Harrington, a gentleman in his sixties, dressed in a grimy three-piece blue pinstripe suit with a white shirt and a monogrammed tie. The clothes had seen better days, but they were Mr Harrington's own and he wore them with as much distinction as possible. He was a former company director whose life had fallen apart after his wife had died three years previously.

She took a seat beside him, feeling the heat of the fire on her face. Old Rosie was murmuring to herself, completely lost in her private world, while Starchy Harris lay asleep against a cardboard box, loud snores issuing from his open mouth.

'Have you dined?' Mr Harrington asked her.

'I had something earlier,' she said.

'I was thinking of taking a small repast. If you'd care to join me.'

From a plastic carrier bag he produced a toasting fork and a packet of beefburgers.

'Fell out of the back of a van,' Mr Harrington said with perfect seriousness. 'I was fortunate that I happened to be passing at the time.' He unwrapped the beefburgers, then stuck two on the prongs of the fork before pushing it into the flames.

Within a few minutes they were sizzling merrily. She expected a scramble for the food, but none of the others around the fire took any interest apart from Mickey Dunn.

'Give us one,' he said.

'These are for Else and I,' Mr Harrington told him. 'You'll wait your turn.'

'I want one now.' Mickey grinned malevolently at them. He was an unstable character, with a temperament that could turn from the pleasant to the vicious in an instant.

But Mr Harrington remained firm. He shook his head, withdrew the fork from the flames.

'Gimme,' said Mickey. 'Now.'

'Certainly not.'

She saw it coming. And so, as Mickey lunged for the fork, she reached out a hand to try to stop him. There was a flurry of movement, and suddenly she felt a prong of the fork plunging deep into her wrist.

She stood up, staggered back, the fork dropping out of her flesh. Mickey and Mr Harrington were also on their

172

feet, Mickey grunting a gruff apology, Mr Harrington concerned that she was all right. Blood was already pulsing out of the gash – red, red blood.

They clustered around her, but she broke free.

'Leave me alone!' she shouted. And then she fled into the night.

She ran until she was out of sight of them, and only then did she stop and lean against the wall. Overhead a mercury lamp enabled her to see the wound in all its grisly glory. An artery had been cut, she knew that, and she was in danger of bleeding to death.

Her overcoat was baggy, and it was easy to roll the sleeve up to her armpit. She removed her belt and tied it around her arm just below the elbow, pulling it as tight as she could.

After a few minutes the bleeding slowed, stopped. She smiled at her success. But she felt light-headed, a bit queasy.

She stumbled on, and came upon a row of semi-derelict shops. She didn't want anyone to see her, but she had to sit down for a while, recover her strength. One of the shops had been boarded up, and it had a deep doorway that was in shadow. She staggered inside, slithered down into a heap in the corner.

The wound was burning, but she couldn't go to hospital. They'd ask questions, want to know who she was. The pain was like fire – it seemed to swirl and pulse. Oh God, she thought, this is my punishment, a judgement for all my sins . . .

The drunk was a big man, built like a lumberjack. And he was swaying gently like a tree about to fall.

'What exactly is the trouble?' Duffy asked him.

They were standing in the waiting area near Susie's

desk. The man had just walked in and began demanding loudly that he wanted attention. Charlie, Megan and Clive were all busy with patients, while Doctor Clarke was in the staff room, complaining that he felt distinctly unwell. Duffy felt a bit like a pebble in the path of a tidal wave.

The man burped loudly in Duffy's face, and she recoiled from the cidery fumes of his breath.

'Puke,' he said. 'Wanna puke.'

Duffy waited nervously, sincerely hoping that he was not going to decorate the waiting area floor. Then he blinked, swallowed and licked his lips.

'Where's the doctor?' he demanded.

'I'm afraid he's not available at the moment,' Duffy said in a tactful manner. 'If you could just tell me what's wrong, then maybe I'll be able to get him.'

The man turned nasty with a suddenness that took Duffy entirely by surprise. Reaching down with his left hand, he grabbed her by the scruff of the neck. At the same time, he delved into the pocket of the donkey jacket he was wearing and produced a garden trowel which he then held in front of her face. Duffy could see that its point had been sharpened.

Despite her terror, Duffy remembered the fortune-teller's warning about bewaring sharp instruments. Somehow the idea that this encounter with the drunk had been fated, helped to calm her a little.

'My dad's got one like that,' she managed to say.

'Eh?' the drunk grunted, his eyelids drooping.

'A trowel,' Duffy said. 'My dad's got one just like that. Says it's great for his parsnips. You do a lot of gardening, do you?'

This was pure invention on her part, but the drunk

frowned, as if giving it some thought. Duffy felt his grip on her uniform slackening.

'He's got this greenhouse as well,' she went on hastily. 'Grows tomatoes. You can hardly keep him out of it.'

'Gardening?' the drunk said quizzically, as though wrestling with some entirely new philosophical concept. 'I don' know nuffin' about gardening.'

'Me, either,' said Duffy. 'Couldn't tell a parsnip from a pineapple.'

After a second, Duffy saw a flicker of amusement on the drunk's bloated face. He was thoroughly plastered, but she'd managed to get through to him and defuse the worst of his blind anger. Now, if she kept humouring him, she might be able to find out why he had come to the hospital.

'Been out celebrating, have you?' she asked. Though he looked older, she reckoned he was in his late twenties. Probably worked in the docks – some sort of job requiring a lot of muscle but not much brain.

She had another reason for keeping him occupied: Susie had phoned for the police when he'd grabbed her. She had to keep him distracted until they arrived.

The drunk burped again, then said, 'My birfday, en't it? Went out wiv some of the lads, an' they filled me up wiv barley wine an' cider. Eighteen pints or more. Need a stomach pump, don' I?'

'Ah,' said Duffy, not quite able to figure out where the sharpened trowel fitted into this scheme of things. But then again, he was probably the kind of hooligan who always carried some sort of offensive weapon around with him. He seemed the type who usually got violent when he was drunk.

'Well, now,' Duffy began, but suddenly she saw Lawrence Clarke come hurrying down the corridor.

'What's going on here?' he was demanding. 'What's all the noise about?'

The drunk had now released Duffy, and he turned to regard Lawrence with hooded eyes.

'Are you a doctor?' he asked.

'Of course I am. And I'm not having any commotion in here.'

Lawrence's brusque manner was like a red rag to a bull. The drunk let out a roar, then grabbed him around the neck with his hand, lifting him up off the floor.

Before he could do anything further, Lawrence suddenly began to twitch in a way that was obviously unconnected with being grabbed. The drunk dropped him, and he fell to his knees, his hands going to his stomach.

'Cramps,' he muttered. And then he began vomiting.

Charlie and Clive were coming down the corridor. The drunk, seeing them, lumbered off, bursting through the door into the children's play area. There was no one inside, but the drunk proceeded to stamp on plastic toys and to hurl a baby walker across the room.

Duffy went to Lawrence Clarke's aid, but he waved her away, still vomiting. Charlie and Clive gingerly approached the play area, where the drunk was now in the process of dismembering a patchwork doll. The patients in the waiting area huddled in the corner, terrified at what was going on.

Suddenly a voice cried, 'Halt!'

It was Stan the porter. He had entered the play area from the other door and was facing the drunk.

'My name is Stanley,' he said, 'and you must be Doctor Livingstone.'

'Eh?' said the drunk.

'I have travelled through dense, hostile jungles to greet you. We must flee – the natives are getting restless.'

The drunk had wrenched off the head of the doll, but now he was just standing there, staring at Stan.

'Yer wot?' he said, looking utterly confused.

'The drums of war are sounding, and we must beat a hasty retreat.'

The drunk looked around, then back at Stan. He blinked. 'Yer bleeding bonkers.'

'My helicopter is waiting,' Stan said. 'Come, we must fly.'

The drunk had started to waver again, but now his eyelids began to droop. He opened his mouth to say something, but at last his intoxication got the better of him. Both his eyes and mouth closed, and then he keeled over.

The loud crash as he hit the floor reverberated throughout the unit. Charlie and Clive were standing in the doorway, staring perplexedly at Stan. As was Duffy. She was wondering if the porter had flipped his lid.

Stan gave a grin and said, 'When someone is mad, it pays to be madder than him, yes?'

Suddenly the entrance doors burst open, and in walked two uniformed police officers with another man dressed in civilian clothing at their head. Duffy recognized him as Ron Naylor, a non-uniformed police officer who often visited the hospital.

'Well, well,' said Charlie. 'Look who it is – the boys in blue. Typical – they always get here when the action's over.'

Naylor, a brawny man in his forties, marched over to him. 'I don't think I like your tone. What's been going on here?'

'We've had a David and Goliath situation,' Charlie told him. He indicated the drunk, now snoring heavily on the floor. 'That's Goliath.' Then he pointed to Stan, who had been dwarfed by the drunk and who was now grinning broadly.

'Don't tell me,' Naylor said, 'his name's David.'

'Wrong,' said Charlie. 'Actually, it's Stan.'

14

She huddled in the doorway, the pain in her hand far worse now. The fire had spread up her arm as far as the tourniquet, but she was tugging hard on the belt to make sure it couldn't get any further. She knew what to do. God wouldn't let her die; He would save her.

Suddenly she became aware that a dog had poked its nose into the shop doorway and was nuzzling her.

'Shoo,' she said weakly. 'Go away.'

It was a scraggly Collie, its eyes a bit wild. Suddenly she was afraid for herself all over again,

'Don't hurt me,' she whimpered. 'Please go away.'

And, as if by magic, the dog withdrew. It paused to cock its leg against the corner of the window, then loped off down the street.

'Thank you,' she murmured. 'Thank you, lord.'

Time passed. She flickered in and out of sleep, and each time she woke the fire in her hand was fiercer. She thought she saw a figure poised briefly in the doorway, staring down at her. But then it was gone.

The rain was coming down heavily now – she could hear it on the street. She liked the rain; it emptied the world of people, filled everything up with its soft sound. Wash me away, she thought, but at the same time she was terrified that she was going to die.

Suddenly a bright light flashed in her face, dazzling her. For a moment she thought that it was an angel, come to carry her up to Heaven. But with a crushing sense of disappointment she realized that it was only a policeman carrying a torch.

She could hear the crackling of his radio, hear him speaking into it. What was he saying? It was something about her, she was sure. She began to feel as if she was drifting in and out of her own body, her thoughts muddled, her senses only intermittently connected with the outside world. But she knew one thing: she was caught at last, tracked down and cornered. They would take her away, lock her up, and she would never be free again.

Baz Samuels straddled her lover on the bed, both of them naked under the single white sheet which she had draped over her shoulders. She moved rhythmically with him, her head thrown back, eyes closed, mouth open. Graham's hands rested on her hips, and she knew he was staring up at her, watching her. But she was only half-aware of him now, too caught up in her own feelings to pay him much heed. The bed rocked gently with their movements, and she could feel herself building inexorably towards the explosive moment of release.

The telephone started ringing.

'Damn it,' she said, slumping forward, her forearms resting on Graham's chest.

'Let it ring,' he said. He was in his thirties, with curly blond hair and brown eyes. In general, Baz liked her men to be slightly older than her.

'No,' she said, 'it might be important.'

Drawing the sheets around her, she reached across to the bedside table and picked up the receiver. She was a striking woman of twenty-eight, with dark hair which fell around her shoulders.

'Hello,' she said into the mouthpiece.

'Barbara?'

She recognized her father's voice with a sense of dismay. There was always a gruff, rather hasty tone to it.

'Hello, dad,' she said without enthusiasm.

'Haven't disturbed you, have I?'

'Well, actually . . .'

'Only it's rather important. I did mention it to you before, but no doubt you've forgotten.'

'Forgotten what?'

'Are you all right? You sound a bit breathless.'

Baz smiled involuntarily and glanced down at Graham.

'I've just run up the stairs,' she told her father.

'Anyway, it's about the finals of the Samuels Cup tomorrow.'

'The Samuels Cup?'

'You know – that youth league thing I sponsored. They're playing the final tomorrow at three o'clock. Your mother and I were hoping you would be there as well.'

'I don't think so, dad.'

'I'd like you to do the presentation. I could introduce you to everyone beforehand. There'll be a few other civic dignitaries there.'

'That'll be nice for me. Want to show me off, do you?'

'Barbara, it does you no harm to make yourself known to people who might be able to help you . . .'

'Father, I'm a doctor, not a prize horse. It's your cup, so you present it.'

'Say you'll come anyway. You told me it was your day off.'

She sighed. 'I've got to go – someone's ringing the doorbell.'

'At ten-thirty at night?'

'It's probably the postman. Deliveries are very late round here, you know.'

181

Grinning, she put the phone down before he could say anything further. Graham was staring across at her.

'My father,' she said. 'Wanting me to be belle of the ball at some football match. Fat chance.'

'What does he do?'

'Owns an engineering firm that makes aircraft components.'

'Not Geoffrey Samuels, is he?'

'That's him.' Her father was well-known in Holby, having always had an eye for self-promotion and for smoothing the feathers of people in local government who could ensure that he maintained a high profile in the public life of the city.

'I'd like to meet him,' Graham said.

'I bet you would.'

'You two don't get on?'

'Not much. He thinks I should be aiming to set myself up in some cushy private practice rather than wasting my time with the NHS. He's always trying to get me to go to these bloody awful functions so that I can chat up the right sort of people. Stuff that.'

Graham stared at her appraisingly. 'I didn't know you were an idealist, Baz.'

'There are some things I believe in strongly. Don't you?'

'In my line of business that's a disadvantage.'

It was the wrong answer, and Baz knew then that this was going to be a one-night stand. Graham ran a successful advertising agency in the city, and he'd been pursuing her for weeks after they'd met at a mutual acquaintance's party. In the end she'd agreed to go out with him because she quite fancied him and because he was entertaining company. But she'd known from the outset that theirs was not going to be a long-term relationship – few of the men in her life had ever been. She valued her independence and preferred to play the field; she didn't want any messy emotional entanglements that might interfere with her career.

Baz was a senior houseman, recently qualified and still serving her time at the City Hospital. She worked the day shift on Casualty, though eventually she hoped to specialize in Orthopaedics. She was enjoying her life at the moment, even though her father's intrusions in it were usually unwelcome.

'What are you thinking?' Graham asked.

'Nothing,' she told him. There was still some pleasure of a physical nature to be had from the evening, and she slid back towards him, saying, 'Now where were we?'

The telephone began ringing again.

'I don't believe it,' she said.

'Pick it up, hang up, then take it off the hook.'

But she knew she wasn't going to do that. Scrambling back over the bed, she snatched up the receiver. 'Baz Samuels.'

'Doctor Samuels?' said a man's voice.

'That's me.'

'I'm Ewart Plimmer, calling from the City Hospital. I was wondering if you could help us out.'

Baz had heard of Ewart Plimmer. His reputation was good, and his case had been a *cause célèbre* at the hospital.

'I'm running the new night shift on the Casualty Department,' he told her, 'and a problem's cropped up. Doctor Clarke, the houseman on duty, has come down with food poisoning.'

'Lawrence Clarke?'

'Yes. He suggested that you might be able to stand in for him.'

183

Baz was surprised to hear this, for she had never got on well with Clarke – he was an arrogant type who wanted to make as much money from his profession as he could. The type of doctor that her father might admire, in fact.

'He recommended me?' she said.

'Yes indeed. We're in rather urgent need of someone. Do you think you could help?'

'I only came off a shift at three o'clock.'

'Yes, I realize that it's an imposition. But you'd be really saving our bacon. We're a bit overwhelmed at the moment.'

Baz was irritated that her evening had been twice interrupted, but Plimmer's politeness and patience began to sway her. He sounded a decent sort, and she'd heard that he was very committed to fighting against hospital cuts.

'All right,' she said, 'I'll be there as soon as I can.'

She put the phone down and began reaching for her bra and panties.

'What are you doing?' Graham asked.

'I've got to go into the hospital. They're short of a doctor in the Casualty Department, so I'm filling in.'

'Now? You're going now?'

She clipped her bra on. 'I could hardly tell them that I need another half hour to finish making love, could I?'

'So what am I going to do?'

'I suggest that you go home and make yourself a cup of cocoa. And have a cold shower, if you need it.'

'That's not very funny.'

'Isn't it?' She slid on a pair of tights. 'I thought it was.'

He climbed out of bed and hurriedly began dressing. She went into the bathroom to freshen up. When she emerged he was fully dressed, his coat on.

'You're angry,' she said.

'Too bloody right I am. It wasn't the way I expected the evening to end.'

This little display of selfishness and petulance irritated her. 'Do you think I'd actually prefer to spend the night dealing with a parade of casualties?'

'It seems like it.'

'Grow up, will you? I'm going in because they need me. Some things are more important than an hour or two of unbridled passion.'

'That's nice to know.'

'There's no need to take it personally.'

'Well, I do.'

He strode towards the door. Now she was even more irritated with him. The typical macho male, she thought, who gets all morose and schoolboyish if he feels that his masculinity's been threatened. Her instincts about him had been right from the start.

He opened the door, then paused. She could see him making an effort to compose himself.

'I'll call you tomorrow,' he said, 'when tempers have cooled.'

'Tempers? I haven't got a temper. I'm just going to work.'

'I'll ring you tomorrow,' he said again.

'Don't bother.'

'What?'

'There's no point. I don't really think we have much to say to one another, do you?'

He stalked out, slamming the door behind him. Baz buttoned up her blouse, a faint smile on her face. She heard Graham's Lotus Elan screech off from the kerbside. It was a red car – very phallic. That should have been warning enough. She could not find in herself a trace of

185

regret that he had gone. And now it was time to get moving herself.

'Two egg sandwiches,' Clyde said nasally, passing the paper bags containing them over the counter.

The bags were stained with translucent grease spots and a smear of ketchup. Andrew Ponting snatched them up, then turned to his partner, Mute. 'It's your turn to pay.'

Both were wearing the dark blue uniform of ambulance personnel, Mute's curly ginger hair bursting out from under her peaked cap. She was as thin as Ponting was plump, and sometimes it seemed to her that they were like some comedy act – Laurel and Hardy in blue.

She fished a pound coin out of her pocket and put it on the counter. Then she and Ponting turned and walked out of the café to their ambulance.

'The standard of service in that establishment has declined,' Ponting said, taking a bite out of his sandwich.

Mute said nothing; she rarely spoke unless she had something interesting or important to say, which was how she had got her nickname. Ponting usually did enough talking for the both of them.

Tonight she was driving while he was the attendant; they usually alternated. As they climbed into the cab, the radio crackled:

'Red Base to Holby 3. Red Base to Holby 5, over.'

Mute put her unopened sandwich down on the dashboard and picked up the radio receiver. 'Holby 5, receiving, over.'

'State your location, please.'

'We're parked in Sydney Road, just outside Max's Café.'

You have an emergency, 54 Raleigh Road. Two students, vomiting and abdominal pains.'

'Roger Red Base.'

Andrew Ponting swallowed another mouthful of egg sandwich. 'That's just around the corner from here, isn't it?'

Mute nodded, starting up the engine and pulling out into the road.

Less than two minutes later they pulled up outside the house, a crumbling Victorian mansion that had long seen better days. A boy and girl in their late teens or early twenties were standing in the doorway, looking anxious.

'Students,' Andrew Ponting said with disgust. He crammed the last of his sandwich into his mouth.

Mute climbed out of the cab and mounted the stone steps which led up to the front door. Ponting followed her, pushing into the front as they confronted the two in the doorway.

Wordless with anxiety, they led Ponting and Mute into the front room of the house. The place was a study in squalor: torn wallpaper, filthy carpets, sleeping bags and old newspapers littering the floor, stale food and cigarette ash everywhere. Mute could see that Ponting would have loved to give the students a lecture on good housekeeping, but this was none of their business and for once he said nothing.

The two students who were ill were lying under the bay window in pools of vomit. The stench was overpowering, and they were groaning and retching while a half-hysterical girl stood over them, waving her arms uselessly.

'It's food poisoning,' one of the students who had been standing in the doorway said emphatically.

'Oh,' said Mute, as Ponting knelt beside them. 'What makes you say that?'

187

'It's that bloody café,' said the girl who was sobbing. 'We all had grub there an hour ago. Are we going to get it as well?'

'What café?' Mute asked, as Ponting looked around anxiously.

'Max's Café,' came the reply.

15

Lawrence Clarke lay groaning on the bed.

'I need something for the pain!' he protested to Baz. Then he retched drily.

'At least your stomach's empty, by the sound of it.'

He glared at her. 'It's not funny.'

'I wasn't trying to be funny.'

'It's agony – the pain!'

'It's not diminishing at all?'

'Well, a little. But I need something. Buscopan.'

'*I'll* do the diagnosing,' she said firmly. 'You're the patient, now.'

'It's food poisoning, isn't that obvious? I've had diarrhoea, abdominal cramps and vomiting. What more do you want?'

Baz bit her lip, resisting the urge to yell at him to shut up and let her get on with her business. She was more edgy than usual because her car had failed to start and she'd had to get a taxi. She had arrived at the hospital late and flustered, and had then been plunged straight into her duties without having the chance even to say hello to the rest of the staff. And Lawrence Clarke was proving more awkward and demanding than most patients.

She was pretty sure that he had a Staphylococcus infection, for which the remedy was simply plenty of fluid and a few days' rest. But he obviously expected special treatment.

189

Baz located Duffy and got her to prepare an intra-muscular injection of an anti-spasmodic and an anti-emetic. Anything for a quiet life.

As this was being done, Charlie Fairhead came up to her.

'We've got two chest pains that need checking,' he said.

'I'll be with you in a moment,' she said.

'You said that ten minutes ago.'

'I've been busy!' she snapped.

'All right, *doctor*,' he said, not disguising his irritation. 'But you're not busy now, are you?'

Bristling, Baz followed him to the cubicle where the first of the two patients was waiting.

Twenty minutes later, they emerged, having agreed that the two patients could be discharged. Both their ECG charts were normal, and indigestion was the likely cause of the pain in both cases. But their ready agreement on diagnosis – Charlie had hinted that he suspected indigestion even before she had examined them – had not lessened the irritation which they felt towards one another.

At this point Ewart came down the corridor. Baz had met him only briefly when she had arrived at the hospital earlier, and they'd scarcely exchanged a dozen words. But he greeted her familiarly enough, and he seemed to sense the hint of discord in the air.

'Problems?' he asked.

'Everything's as sweet as honey,' Charlie said wryly.

'Thanks for coming in,' Ewart said to Baz. 'Coping?'

'Just about.'

'We've got our hands full tonight. Two more food poisoning cases have just come in.'

They headed down the corridor towards the ambulance bay.

'Meet Ponting and Mute,' Charlie said to Baz, introducing her to the ambulance man and woman who had just brought in the stretchered patients.

The woman nodded at Baz as she leaned over to examine one of the patients, but the man was looking worried.

'They reckon they picked it up at Max's Café,' he was saying to Ewart. 'I'd only just finished eating an egg sandwich from there. The place has gone to the dogs – something ought to be done about it.'

'We've got another call,' Mute said.

They hurried off. Charlie took one of the stretchers, pointing it down the corridor in the direction of the cubicles. Baz took the other.

'Didn't Lawrence mention that he'd eaten at Max's before coming in?' Ewart asked.

'He did,' said Charlie. 'That's our connection.'

'This is a notifiable illness,' Ewart said. 'I'd better ring the Health Officer.'

He headed off towards his office. As Baz and Charlie reached the cubicles with their stretcher, Stan appeared.

'Where were you when we needed you?' Charlie said to him.

'Busy,' he said, 'carrying a woman besieged by the Devil to our Angels of Mercy.' He glanced at Baz. 'You have come to help us in our hour of need?'

'Something like that,' she said. 'Who's being besieged by the Devil?'

Then they heard the screaming; a woman's voice, yelling, 'Keep away! Keep away!'

* * *

Megan had gone numb with shock and surprise when the woman had first been brought in, but she quickly recovered her composure. Alice Biley had a thin silver belt tied tight around her arm, and her hand was puffed up like a balloon. She was delirious, raving.

'Keep away!' she screamed at Megan and Clive as they tried to approach her. 'Armageddon! The last battle for my soul!'

'It's all right,' Clive said gently. 'We're here to help you.'

'Agents of Satan!' Alice yelled. 'Servants of Mephistopheles, dressed in white to lure the unsuspecting sinner to damnation!'

'No,' Clive said. 'We're nurses. You're in hospital.'

'Keep back, or God will strike you down!'

Clive glanced helplessly at Megan. She was still shocked by Alice's appearance, shocked by her mania. But she had to try to do something.

'Alice,' she said softly.

Alice looked directly upwards, as if someone overhead had spoken. 'Who calls me?'

'It's me. Your old friend, Megan.'

Slowly her gaze descended from the ceiling to focus on Megan. Her eyes were bright and wild, her pupils dilated.

'Remember me?' Megan said. 'We used to be nurses together.'

'Sin of sins!' Alice cried. 'She died in blood, crucified in her bed, abandoned by the scarlet woman.'

'You're safe here now. We want to help you.'

'A mortal sin, and there will be punishment!'

Alice was cowering on the bed, and Megan slowly edged towards it.

'We were friends,' she said. 'Close friends.'

'God abandons those who betray him. He leaves them alone, casts them out to perish in the wild.'

'That's how I know your name. It's Alice Biley, isn't it?'

'Death. That's all that awaits. Death and eternal damnation.'

'Alice?'

At last Alice looked at her, and Megan thought she detected a flicker of recognition in those wild eyes.

'Let me help you,' she said. 'Will you?'

She moved even closer to the bed. Alice did not react, but there was still the cornered expression in her face. Her swollen hand was resting in her lap, and she was still gripping the belt around her arm tightly.

'You do remember me, don't you?' Megan said.

Alice was silent, staring at her. Tentatively Megan reached out towards her hand. 'Can I have a look at it?'

'No!' Alice yelled, snatching the hand away from her. 'God and the Devil are in that hand. They are fighting a battle for my soul.'

Megan glanced at Clive, who was sensibly standing near the door, making no move to approach.

'I see,' she said to Alice. 'Then we must be very careful. I won't hurt it.'

Alice shook her head violently, huddling in the corner of the bed. Her hair was filthy, her overcoat stained with blood. Megan remembered her as she had been: smart, active, efficient. Now she was like a trapped animal.

'I'll be back,' Clive said, and then he slipped out of the cubicle.

Megan stepped back a little, giving Alice a bit of room.

'We need to take the belt off,' she said conversationally. 'You know that, Alice, don't you?'

'No! Without it, the Devil would travel straight up to

my heart, and then it would all be over! I have to keep him trapped in my hand.'

'If you don't let us look at it, you'll die.'

'God will save me, if I'm worthy. I must trust in him!'

'Please, Alice.'

She moved forward again, but Alice screamed at her to keep back.

Megan felt utterly helpless. The policeman who'd found Alice lying in a shop doorway had radioed for an ambulance, and she had been raving when she was brought in. Everything pointed to the fact that she had been lying in the doorway for a few hours at least, with the tourniquet tight around her arm. Unless the hand was soon attended to, she might lose it – and her life as well.

The cubicle door opened, and Clive walked in with Doctor Ferguson – the on-duty psychiatrist. He was a tall, swarthy man with dark eyes which twinkled behind his horn-rimmed glasses.

'Satan!' Alice screamed at him. 'God will protect me from you!' She began spitting and snarling at him while scrambling against the wall as if trying to burrow through it and escape.

'What's the background here?' Dr Ferguson asked quickly.

Megan gave him all the details while he stared at Alice and she yelled at him to begone.

'She won't take the belt off?' he asked.

'No,' Megan said. 'She claims the Devil's in her hand and that he'll attack her heart if she removes it.'

Ferguson was a brisk, quick-thinking type who seldom lingered over therapeutic decisions.

'Right,' he said, 'there's nothing for it. We're going to have to sedate her. Diazepam injection, ten milligrams.'

It was the maximum dosage. Clive departed to prepare

194

the injection, while Megan attempted to pacify Alice once more with words. But she was too far gone now, too much in terror of Doctor Ferguson, who simply stood there, peering hard at her through his glasses. Megan thought she detected a hint of impatience in his face, as if he knew it was futile to attempt to reason with her in her present condition. And in a way he was right; Alice was no longer in touch with the real world, and until her delirium had been dealt with, there was no reasoning with her. But that couldn't stop Megan from trying.

'Alice,' she said, 'you remember me, don't you? Megan. Megan Roach.'

Alice was staring hard at Doctor Ferguson like a lamb might eye a stalking lion.

'Remember the time we went to Weston-super-Mare for the day?' Megan said, desperately trying to stir some memory in her. 'We bought ice-creams and paddled in the sea.'

Alice turned to her, and for a moment Megan thought that she finally recognized her. Then she said, 'He is the Devil, and you are his servant.' She turned back to Doctor Ferguson and yelled, 'Begone, foul demon! The Lord is my protector and salvation!'

Doctor Ferguson remained calm, unmoved by her imprecations. Utterly professional, Megan thought, not getting emotionally involved. But it wasn't that easy for her.

Clive returned with the hypodermic. Megan immediately felt a mixture of relief and apprehension.

'We're going to give you an injection,' Clive said.

'No!' Alice screamed. 'Keep back!'

'It'll make you feel better,' Ferguson said, as Clive moved forward.

Alice let out a blood-curdling shriek and went into a

foetal huddle. She began to rock rapidly to and fro on the bed.

'You'll have to hold her down,' Ferguson told Megan.

It was what Megan had been dreading, but she knew that there was nothing for it.

Without further ado, she pinioned Alice against the mattress. Alice began to flail and writhe, screaming for God to save her.

Megan couldn't look at her face. Her overcoat had fallen open to reveal the stained and faded floral dress she was wearing underneath. On her legs were thick black nylon tights, laddered and holed in many places. As she twisted around in the bed, Clive ripped one of the legs of the tights open, exposing a thigh muscle.

It was degrading, but Megan knew there was no alternative. As Clive swabbed Alice's skin preparatory to administering the injection, she surged upright in the bed, staring straight at Megan.

'Help me!' she cried. 'Don't let Satan steal my soul!'

For an instant Megan wavered, wanting to prove to her that she was still her friend. Then her nurse's training reasserted itself, and she clamped her ankles firmly to the mattress and forced her shoulders back on to the pillow. Alice let out a long, terrible scream as Clive slid the needle home.

16

'They've all eaten sausages,' Baz told Ewart as they walked down the corridor with Charlie. 'That seems to be the connection. Max's Café, and sausages.'

'Max isn't going to like it,' Charlie said.

'If it's his sausages that caused it,' said Ewart, 'then he's only got himself to blame.'

'Not necessarily,' Charlie replied. 'He's had temporary staff standing in for the past few days while his wife's been in hospital. She's had a gallstone op. In fact, I think he's upstairs with her now.'

'Whether he was there or not,' Ewart pointed out, 'he'll still be legally accountable.'

Baz said, 'Jumping the gun a bit, aren't we? We don't know for certain that his place is to blame.'

They passed the ambulance bay. Mute was standing impatiently by the doors, while Ponting sat on a chair, listening aghast to Stan:

'Nineteen fifty-eight, it was. August. A beautiful summer. Poznan. That is where I lived before I came to England. Terrible it was, people keeling over like bluebottles, yes? Foaming in the mouths, twitching all over.'

'Epileptic fits?' Ponting said hopefully.

'Food poisoning,' Stan said with relish. 'Their hair fell out, and then their nails, and then their teeth.'

'My God!' said Ponting, surging to his feet. 'Someone's going to pay for this!'

He hurried out, closely followed by Mute, who was

grinning to herself. Charlie walked over to Stan, who also had a smile on his face – a smile of satisfaction.

'You ought to be ashamed of yourself,' Charlie told him. 'Frothing at the mouth and hair falling out – I've never heard anything like it.'

'That is what I was told.'

'What do you mean? Weren't you there?'

'I was on holiday at the time – visiting my uncle in Lodz. When I went home afterwards, everyone was talking about it. All the graphic details, yes?'

'But Ponting thinks you actually saw it.'

'He is always jumping to conclusions, that man. He thinks he is going to suffer horribly, but it is plain as noses on faces that nothing is wrong with him at all.'

'So you were just reporting what you'd been told.'

'That is correct, Mr Charlie.'

'You old rogue. You were just trying to put the willies up him, weren't you?'

'I know no one called Willie,' Stan said, straight-faced. 'But I do know our Sergeant Ronald Naylor.'

'He was here?'

Stan nodded. 'He was most interested to hear Ponting talk of the food poisoning and of Max's Café. He has gone off to have words with the people there.'

'Damm it,' Ewart said, 'it's the Environment Health Officers' business to do enquiries in these cases, not the police's.'

'You know Naylor,' said Charlie. 'Loves to play the heavy cop.'

'Do you think Ponting may fall ill after all?' Stan asked. He sounded almost hopeful.'

Charlie grinned. 'No love lost between you two, is there?'

'His partner, Mute, is a nice person. Once I gave her

flowers. He laughed at me, called me a fool. But there is
no bigger fool than him. The louder the mouth, the emptier
the head is what my grandmother always told me. In Polish,
of course.' He giggled. 'I do not wish him any great harm
– some rumblings of the stomach and many visits to the
gentlemen's convenience would be sufficient. But I think I
have perhaps put the wind up him, yes?'

Then he sauntered cheerfully off, whistling a tune that
none of them knew.

'You've got some characters here,' Baz remarked to
Ewart.

'Indeed we have. Makes the job a bit more interesting,
wouldn't you say?'

She glanced at him. 'I have the feeling that you're
trying to get at something.'

'Well,' he said, 'I was wondering.'

'What?'

'If perhaps you'd be interested in joining the staff on a
permanent basis . . .'

'Not me.'

'I don't think Lawrence Clarke will be wanting to
after he's recovered. And frankly, my feeling is that he
wouldn't fit in here particularly well.'

'I'd have to agree with you there. He's not the self-
sacrificing type.'

'Whereas you strike me as having the right attitude.
And I've heard that you're pretty good at your job as
well.'

'Oh?' said Baz, glancing at Charlie. 'Who told you
that?'

'Not me,' Charlie said. 'As far as I'm concerned, you've
still got it all to prove.'

She knew that he was teasing her a little, but she took

the comment seriously. To Ewart she said, 'Are they all as cocksure as this one?'

Ewart merely smiled, refusing to take sides.

Suddenly they heard shrieks from the waiting area. A girl in her teens was running around, tearing at her hair, knocking over chairs, and shouting, 'They're after me! The walls are after me! Keep them away!'

Clive and another nurse were pursuing her, while other waiting patients stared with a mixture of horror and indifference. An elderly woman with no visible injuries was knitting a long black and white scarf which hung down on the floor; she was oblivious of everything else around her. A young girl with a gash on her knee sat prodding the wound with her finger, displaying no apparent pain. A man with an injury to his right arm was vainly trying to turn the pages of a magazine which sat on his knee; he winced with the slightest movement. A short man who was blissfully drunk had just unzipped himself and was about to urinate in a waste-paper bin against the wall.

'Oh no you don't!' Charlie said, rushing over to him and grabbing him by the scruff of the neck and carrying him off helter-skelter down the corridor to the gents.

Clive and the nurse had cornered the girl, who was now whimpering with terror. Several of the patients were egging them on, shouting 'Go on, get her!' while others were equally adamant that she should be left alone. A typical cross-section of casualties, Baz thought, ranging from the sublime to the ridiculous. All human life was here, most of it in the raw.

Clive approached the girl gingerly, saying 'It's all right, it's all right.' Susie stepped out from behind her desk, holding a small crumpled paper bag which she offered to

200

Ewart and Baz. Indicating the girl, she said, 'This fell out of her pocket.'

Baz opened it up. Inside were several withered brown fungi.

'Magic mushrooms,' Ewart said. 'The first of the season.'

The girl, somewhat pacified, was led off by Clive towards a cubicle for treatment. Charlie reappeared, leading the drunk back to his seat.

'There was a fire in that waste-paper basket,' the drunk was saying to Charlie. 'I was only trying to put it out.'

'Tell us another one,' Charlie replied, plonking him down on a seat. 'Now you just sit there and behave yourself until you're called.'

'I'll go and have a look at the girl,' Ewart said to Baz. 'And check on these mushrooms with the Poisons Centre.'

'I thought you were supposed to be taking a back seat on the treatment side,' Baz said.

'Personal interest,' Ewart told her.

'You know the girl?'

'No, but I know someone like her who had a fling with these. Lots of pretty lights and colours, but often a good dose of paranoia, too.'

He went off. Charlie, who had overheard the conversation, said, 'I bet he's talking about his daughter.'

'Does he have problems with her?'

'Well, she's not a drug addict as far as I know. But I don't think things are going that great with his family. He seems a bit – distracted to me tonight. I know the feeling.'

Baz glanced at him, wondering what he meant. But there was no opportunity to say anything for Duffy suddenly came hurrying down the corridor.

'Doctor,' she said, 'in cubicle five. We've got a cardiac arrest.'

* * *

The café was empty of customers, so Morton and Clyde were taking a breather. They sat on bar stools behind the counter, playing cards.

'Snap,' said Morton as Clyde put down a Mrs Pig.

'This is stupid,' Clyde grumbled as Morton gathered up the cards.

'I know.' Morton wiped his nose on the sleeve of his tunic. 'But it was the only pack I could find.'

'This is a lark, eh?'

'What?'

'This game.'

'Snap?'

'No, this restaurant lark. Ever done it before?'

'Never. I was training to be a brickie, only the course was shut down. You still fiddling about with motorbikes?'

'Now and then. Max don't know then that you've never been a chef?'

'Naw. My uncle told him I'd worked at the Argyll Hotel in the High Street, under the chef there. I did, for a week. Emptied the slop bins.' He sniffed. 'What did you tell him?'

'Said I worked for MacDonald's, didn't I? Well, I did clean the windows there once.'

They exchanged lop-sided grins.

The door opened, and in walked a middle-aged man in a crumpled grey suit.

'What can we do for you?' Morton asked amiably as he approached the counter.

'You can close this bloody place down right away, for a start.' The man reached into the inside pocket of his jacket and produced identification. 'Detective Sergeant Naylor.'

'What's up?' asked Morton.

'A lot of food, that's what's up – all over the floor of

the Casualty Department at the hospital. Food poisoning, that's what's up. And it looks like this place is to blame.'

Morton and Clyde exchanged glances, then both of them guiltily hid their grubby fingers from sight under the counter.

The door opened again, and in walked two students, a boy and a girl, both tall and dressed in faded denims.

'Gerroutofit!' Naylor yelled at them, stopping them in their tracks. 'This place is closed.'

'It says OPEN on the door,' the girl told him.

Naylor stalked over to them, flashing his police identification card. 'See this? This says it's closed.'

The boy and girl did not bother to argue; they turned and walked out, the boy murmuring something to the girl before they slammed the door behind them.

'What did he say?' Naylor asked Morton and Clyde.

'Sounded like "fascist pig",' Clyde informed him.

'Very funny.'

'It wasn't a jo – '

'Now listen to me. I'm going off to contact the Public Health Inspector. He'll be wanting to give this place a thorough going over. After I'm gone, I want that door locked behind me. You're not to serve food to *anyone*, is that clear?'

'D'you know what caused it then?' Morton asked.

'Not a bloody food poisoning expert, am I? That's for the Health Inspector to decide. Judging by the state of this place, it could be every bloody thing. While I'm away, I don't want anything touched or moved, is that understood?'

He glared at Morton and Clyde until they both nodded.

'You're coming back then?' said Clyde.

'Course I bloody am. And if I find that anything's been

203

moved or cleaned up, I'm going to have both of your guts for garters. You just stay where you are, and wait.'

Naylor went out, closing the door behind him. Morton and Clyde looked at one another.

'This is a bit of a pisser,' Morton said.

Clyde scratched a boil on his bum. 'What are we going to do?'

'First of all, we shut up shop. Then we're going to sling out everything that's left in the kitchen and clean it all down.'

'You mean get rid of it?'

'Ten out of ten. That way they won't be able to pin anything on us, will they?'

'But what about the copper?'

'He's got no evidence. And we can make sure that he can't find any when he gets back.'

Morton was already moving towards the door. But as he reached it, the door burst open.

In stormed Andrew Ponting.

'You two!' he said, pointing a beefy finger at them, 'you served us egg sandwiches tonight.'

'I didn't eat mine,' Mute said, coming in behind him.

Ponting glared briefly at her, then returned his attention to Morton and Clyde. 'We've got half the city down with food poisoning . . .'

'That's an exaggeration,' Mute said.

'Will you shut up?' he said to her. 'Just look at this pair! Not exactly Mr and Mrs Clean, are they? This place is probably crawling with salmonella.'

'Nothing to do with us,' Morton said.

'Don't give me that! Look at your clothes, your hands. Like a pair of dustmen, you are.'

Ponting was Welsh, and his accent and phrasing always became more pronounced when he was angry. 'I'll bloody murder you, I will! If I come down with food poisoning from that sandwich, I'll crawl back here on my hands and knees and throttle the pair of you!'

Mute was cocking an ear to the ambulance, which was parked just outside. A muffled voice was coming over the radio.

'We've got a call,' she said to Ponting. 'Come on, let's go.'

'Not till I've finished giving this pair a piece of my mind. Look at them! A shambles, they are.'

'There's nothing wrong with you,' Morton said.

'Not yet, there isn't. But food poisoning can take hours to come on. And the first rumble I get, I'll be back here to sort you out!'

Mute had already departed to answer the call. He stormed after her. Seconds later, the ambulance screeched off into the night.

'Phew!' said Clyde. 'That was a close shave.'

'Maybe we ought to change the name of this place,' Morton remarked. 'Call it Montezuma's Revenge.'

He chuckled at his joke, but Clyde was looking at him blankly.

'Who's Monty Zoomer?' he asked.

'Just lock the bloody door, will you?'

Clyde swung it shut and dropped the latch. He turned the sign around so that it said CLOSED, then drew the net curtain on the window.

'Funny thing is,' he said to Morton, 'I've been feeling a bit queasy myself in the last half-hour. Do you think it's that dinner you cooked for us?'

'Listen,' Morton said, 'I made sure my hands were clean for that one. And the pans as well. Now come on, and let's get the kitchen spick and span.'

But before they could move, there was a hammering on the door.

'Bloody hell,' said Morton, 'this place is popular all of a sudden.' In a louder voice he shouted: 'We're closed!'

'You're not closed to me!' came the reply.

Morton and Clyde stared at one another. The voice belonged to none other than Max himself.

Clyde opened the door, and Max marched inside.

Hastily Morton said, 'How's your missus?'

'She's fine,' Max said through clenched teeth. 'Which is more than you pair are going to be.'

Morton pretended innocence. 'What's up?'

'You know damn well what's up. I got a message from the Casualty Department while I was at the hospital. About people coming in with food poisoning. People who'd been eating here earlier.'

He had walked up to the counter and ran his finger over it. It came away smudged black with dust and grime.

'This place is a disgrace,' he said to them. 'I've only been away for two days, and it looks like a pig-sty.'

'We've been overworked . . .' Morton began.

'I don't want to hear any excuses. I don't want to hear *anything* from you – I can see for myself.'

He went through into the kitchen, Morton and Clyde following him trepidatiously. He stared in silence for long moments before finally saying, 'Bloody disgusting.'

The place was a mess, with gravy stains and lumps of grease over all the work surfaces, unwashed pans piled high beside the sink, towers of filthy, teetering crockery everywhere. Grubby dishcloths and tea-towels hung from cupboard-door handles or wallowed in pools of congealing spaghetti sauce. On the floor were bits of bacon rind, eggshells, lumps of bread, squashed baked beans and dollops of tomato.

'We were just about to start cleaning up,' Morton said.

'What do you take me for?' Max replied without looking at him. 'I can recognize incompetence when it's staring me in the face. The mistake I made was in thinking you pair could muddle through for a couple of days while I was away.'

He went over to the refrigerator and pulled open the heavy door. Inside a similar chaos prevailed, packs of bacon stacked on top of cartons of mushrooms, frozen lamb chops defrosting slowly over a tub of dripping, a jug of milk sitting directly underneath segments of uncooked black pudding. And finally, there was a trade pack of pork and beef sausages whose cellophane wrapping had been split wide open. Immediately above it was a hunk of steak which had evidently been flash-fried before being put back in the fridge. Blood was dripping from the steak, seeping into the sausages below.

'Listen,' Morton said to Max, 'we can get rid of this lot, clean up everything before the Health Inspector gets here. They wouldn't have anything to pin on us.'

Max turned to look at him with an expression of undisguised distaste.

'That's not my way of doing things,' he said. 'Never has been. There's a dozen sick people in that hospital – sick because of what's been going on here. I like to face up to my responsibilities, and I'm going to now.'

'They'll close you down.'

'And I'll have you to thank for that. But it's important they know exactly what caused it, and I'm going to make sure they get every opportunity to find out.'

Clyde was looking distinctly off-colour. 'Did they say what might have caused it?' he asked.

'They did,' Max told him. 'And I'm pretty sure they're

right.' He pointed to the blood dripping down on the sausages.

'No,' said Clyde. 'Not sausages, was it?'

Max simply nodded.

'Bloody hell,' said Morton. 'Our dinner. It was toad in the hole!'

Clyde began to heave.

17

Charlie poured milk into the coffees for himself and Baz. He sat down beside her, putting his feet up on the edge of the table. Through the window behind them, the pale light of dawn was colouring the sky.

'Well,' said Charlie, 'that's the first night almost over. What did you think of it?'

Baz had a pen in her hand and her Casualty Cards spread out in front of her, ready for completion. But she wasn't writing anything.

'I should have saved that Arrest,' she said. 'I don't understand why he died on me.'

Charlie looked at her. 'Hey, you did all you could. He was getting on a bit, with a past history.'

'He was only fifty-three.'

Charlie was truly surprised that she had mentioned the man. He had helped Baz in her attempts to revive him, and she had worked hard giving him heart massage and defillibration before the crash team took over. Twice she'd got his heart going after it had stopped, but the third time he hadn't revived, despite all her efforts.

At the time she'd been brisk and businesslike about the man's death, simply saying, 'Well, that's it,' and then getting on to her next patient. Which was all a doctor could do in such circumstances since they were there to heal the living, not mourn over the dead. But now it was as if her remorse had simply been deferred until later.

Charlie did not like this idea. He had been impressed by the effort and expertise which she had put into attempting to stabilize the man's heart, and his opinion of her as a doctor had been revised upwards considerably. But that was in strictly medical terms. It was also necessary to have the right temperament to cope with the tragic deaths which were always going to be part and parcel of their work. You had to be considerate, sympathetic but ultimately tough-minded, otherwise you'd just end up being overwhelmed by grief.

'He'd had two previous heart attacks,' Charlie said, 'and he was also overweight and a heavy smoker. Apparently he'd took no notice of warnings to change his lifestyle, get more exercise and cut down on the fags.'

Almost unknown to himself, Charlie had lit up a cigarette. He stared at it, feeling a bit of a hypocrite. Baz was still silent.

'Listen,' he said, 'these things happen. Haven't you ever had a patient die on you before?'

'You know who he reminded me of?' she said abruptly.

'Who?'

'My Uncle Maurice. It was like seeing him all over again. He had a fatal heart attack, too, when I was eight years old. On the seventeenth hole of a golf course. I was with him at the time.'

'You were with him?'

'He used to take me with him sometimes, and I'd go looking for his golf balls if they got lost in the rough. He was my favourite uncle.'

Charlie waited, knowing more was coming.

'I remember him lying there, turning purple. I was petrified. There was another man with us, and he rushed off to phone an ambulance. I was left there, staring at him, not knowing what to do. He didn't say anything, and his eyes were closed. I wanted to run away, to hide myself somewhere, but I couldn't move.'

She shuffled the cards in her hands, staring blindly down at them. 'He was dead by the time the ambulance-men arrived. And that was when I decided that I wanted to be a doctor.' She looked across at Charlie. 'Oh, I know it probably sounds terribly dramatic, but I remember thinking "I've got to find a way of doing something to help people when they get ill". That was the start of it, really.'

Charlie drew on his cigarette. When it was clear she wasn't going to say anything further, he said, 'No wonder you took it a bit hard. Can't say I blame you.'

'Well, it's all over now, isn't it? Give us a cigarette, will you?'

He offered her the pack. 'I didn't know you smoked.'

'Only now and then – when I really feel I need it.' She took a light off the end of his cigarette. 'Terrible habit. What a bad example we'd be setting if the patients could see us.'

'We're only human, like them.'

'Too true.' She squinted at him through the smoke. 'Thanks.'

'For what?'

'You know – for listening.'

'Pity you're not going to be joining us on a permanent basis,' Charlie said. 'We could use you around here.'

At this point the door opened and in walked Clive.

'How's the magic mushroom girl?' Charlie asked him.

'She's got a headache,' he replied, 'but otherwise she's fine.'

'Parents arrived yet to give her a rollicking?'

'That's the funny thing – *they* gave her the mushrooms. They're a pair of ageing hippies who reckoned she needed a bit of psychedelic enlightenment.'

'You're kidding,' said Baz.

211

Clive shook his head. 'Throwbacks to the 'sixties, the pair of them. Kept calling me *man* and saying things were *heavy*. I expected them to hand me a flower at any minute.'

Clive began to put his jacket on.

'You're not staying for a coffee?' Charlie asked.

'No, I have to get back, grab as much sleep as possible. Got the big game this afternoon – the Samuels Cup. You coming?'

'I'll do my best,' Charlie told him.

'Did you say the Samuels Cup?' Baz asked.

Clive nodded. 'This guy who sponsored it any relation of yours?'

'Sort of,' she said with a little grin.

'So you'll be coming, too?'

'I don't know the first thing about football, apart from the fact that you have to use your feet. But I thought the Cup was a junior league thing, for kids.'

'It is. I'm the trainer of one of the teams, the St Andrews Strollers. My two boys play in the side.'

'Well,' said Baz, 'I hope you win.'

Clive departed. As he went out, Duffy entered.

'How's the food poisonings?' Charlie asked her.

'They'll survive,' she said. 'Most of them are over the worst.'

'How many did we get altogether?' asked Baz.

'Fourteen,' Duffy told her. 'The last two we had in were a right pair of dingbats.'

'They were Max's temporary staff,' Charlie said, 'the ones who actually caused the trouble in the first place, as far as we can tell.'

'Well, they've been moaning and groaning ever since they were brought in. They're both convinced they're going to die, even though they've stopped vomiting.'

'Poetic justice,' said Charlie. 'But I feel sorry for poor old Max.'

'Will they close him down?' Duffy asked.

'Probably, for a while, at least. But if I know him, he'll take it on the nose. And once he's back in operation, I'll be giving him my custom again as a sign of good faith.'

'Me, too,' said Duffy. 'I couldn't do without his doughnuts.'

'Doughnuts,' said Baz. 'I could murder one of those right now.'

'There's a café just down the road that opens at seven,' Charlie said. 'They'll have cakes and buns in from the bakery, straight out of this morning's oven. I'll treat you to breakfast, if you like.'

Baz peered at him. 'Are you trying to bribe me into staying with the shift?'

'It's worth thinking about. But there's no strings attached.'

'OK,' said Baz, 'you're on. But I warn you – you won't change my mind.'

Duffy had taken an object wrapped in blue paper from her pocket.

'What's that?' Charlie asked.

She unwrapped it to reveal the garden trowel with which the drunk had threatened her several hours earlier.

'What do you want that for?' Charlie asked her.

'As a memento of my first night on the shift,' she told him. 'And also as proof that things really are written in the stars.'

'I'm not with you.'

'I saw this fortune-teller a while back, and she warned me to beware sharp instruments.'

'Did she know you were a nurse?'

Duffy nodded. 'I know what you're going to say – it's

213

obvious that I'm going to encounter sharp instruments if I'm working in a hospital. But Madame Natasha also predicted that I'd meet Mr Plimmer and that my life would be changed. And it has.'

'Madame Natasha, eh?' said Baz. 'Sounds very exotic.'

'Actually,' Duffy admitted, 'she looked more like Flo the Floor-Cleaning Lady.'

Duffy's giggle was infectious, and both Charlie and Baz smiled. She made herself a coffee, diluting it heavily with milk and drinking it down quickly. Then she studied the trowel again.

'Maybe I ought to use it as a weapon as well,' she mused, 'to keep my boyfriend in line.'

'Have trouble with him, do you?' said Baz.

'He's a right pain, sometimes. Always messing me about.'

'Treat 'em rough,' said Baz. 'That's the only answer.'

She was half-joking, but her comment was sufficient to start Charlie thinking about Liz. He had busied himself with his work all night, staving off thoughts of her, but he knew that they had a lot to sort out and that it was likely to be messy. Or would she simply have upped and gone by the time he'd gone home, taking all her stuff with her? Liz could sometimes be impulsive yet firm in her decisions, and the idea was far from impossible.

'Charlie?' said Duffy.

'Eh? What?'

'I said – has Megan home home yet?'

'No,' Charlie said. 'She's upstairs, visiting one of the patients – an old friend of hers, apparently.'

Baz was scrutinizing him. 'You look as if you've just seen a ghost.'

'Not seen, exactly,' he replied, thinking again of Liz. 'But you might be right about it being a ghost.'

* * *

Alice lay in a bed next to the window at the end of the ward, having been moved there from Casualty several hours earlier. There were screens around the bed, but no doctors or nurses were attending her.

'Her condition's stable,' the Ward Sister told Megan as she led her to the bed. 'With proper care she should make a good recovery.'

Megan paused before stepping behind the screen. She stared down the ward. It was in the Geriatric wing, the only place where a bed had been free at the time. A few of the patients were asleep, but most were busily tucking into their breakfast, chattering to the nurses and to one another as they did so. The gossipy atmosphere helped dispel some of Megan's forebodings.

'She's heavily sedated,' the Ward Sister said, 'and she may not wake.'

'I know,' Megan said. 'I just wanted to see her for a few minutes.'

'Of course. I'll leave you to it.'

She departed, striding briskly off down the ward. Megan hesitated, then stepped inside the screen.

Alice had been dressed in a white gown, and she lay peacefully asleep on an equally white pillow. Her face had been cleaned of its grime, and her hair, though still filthy, had been combed.

Her condition had improved dramatically since she had been sedated, and her hand, now bound with bandages, looked scarcely swollen at all. Ragged breaths came from her half-open mouth, but they were steady, regular breaths. She was going to be all right. Medically, at least.

A drip fed clear liquid into her left arm. Antibiotics in a saline solution. Megan sat down in a chair beside the bed, not taking her eyes off her friend's face. Oddly, she felt none of the anguish which she had experienced earlier. Alice was safe now. Safe and stable.

She reached out and grasped her unbandaged hand between her own. Her fingers felt like bent sticks in dry leather pouches. She looked twenty years older than her true age. Megan tried to think of all the things they had done together when they had been young, but at that moment her mind was blank. Sunlight slanted on to the lower half of the bed, on the pale green weave of the coverlet.

'Megan.'

With a start, she saw that Alice was awake and staring at her through very drowsy eyes. But she had spoken her name, and Megan was relieved to see that the brittle gleam of mania was gone from her eyes.

'How are you, Alice?' she said softly.

'Very tired. I did a silly thing.'

'You're all right now.'

'Will they lock me away, Megan? I've done terrible things.'

'No one's going to lock you away. We all want to look after you.'

'I thought the Devil had got into my hand.'

'You were delirious. You nearly died. But everything's going to be all right now, I promise.'

'This is a hospital, isn't it?'

'The City Hospital. You'll be comfy here for a few days. They'll feed you and look after you.'

Alice ran a tongue over her dry lips. 'I don't suppose they'll give me any gin.'

Megan smiled, both with relief and amusement. The fact that Alice had shown a hint of humour indicated that she was already making a good recovery.

'What you need most now is rest,' she said. 'Rest and plenty of good food.'

'Pity I'm in hospital then. You don't get much rest in hospitals, do you? And we all know what the food's like.'

Again Megan smiled. 'You're ex-staff. You can insist on the best.'

Alice shook her head, slowly but firmly. 'Don't tell them I used to be a nurse. I'd be ashamed.'

Megan swallowed a lump in her throat. 'All right,' she said. 'All right.'

'I've been living rough, you know. For years. Wandering the streets.'

'Haven't you got a place of your own?'

'Oh, yes. A whole council house. It's boarded up, but I found a way of sneaking in. You won't tell anyone, will you?'

'Not if you don't want me to. But if you haven't got any money or a proper place to live, there's organizations to help you . . .'

'Busybodies.'

'Don't be daft,' Megan said bluntly. 'This is the Welfare State, remember?'

'What's left of it. People like me slip through the net.'

Megan leaned forward. 'You have to let me help you, Alice. I want to. We can get you somewhere decent to live for a start.'

'I'm tired.'

'Will you think about it? And let me know when I see you next time?'

'You're coming back, are you?'

'I'll visit every day – if you want me to.'

Alice was silent.

'Not as a busybody,' Megan said, 'but as a friend.'

The lids had drooped on Alice's eyes, but now they

217

flickered open again. She said, 'You couldn't sneak us i a drop of gin, could you?'

'Definitely not,' Megan said firmly. 'Not a drop.'

'Some friend you are.'

But it was said in a slightly bantering tone. Mega rose. 'I'll see you tomorrow then.'

'Don't bring grapes. I'm allergic to them.'

Megan smiled and stepped through the screen. As sh was leaving she heard Alice murmur, 'I've never mucl liked beefburgers, either.'

She let this cryptic comment go unchallenged an departed. It was going to be difficult to get Alice to accep any help from other people, but she was determined t try. Otherwise Alice would just drift back to an alcoholi life on the road and would be trapped in a downwar spiral once more. But Megan was pleased that she' actually recognized her and responded to her. It was big start.

Outside the ward, someone hailed her. It was Terry Breen. He walked up to her, beaming.

'Thanks,' he said in a voice rich with gratitude. 'Thank for your advice.'

Megan blinked, desperately trying to think of wha advice she had given him.

'I told her the joke,' Terry said.

'The joke?'

'About the porcupine and the chimpanzee. Mandy She loved it.'

'She did?'

Terry nodded vigorously. 'She laughed and laughed. Then I told her lots of others, too. Afterwards she said that I was really funny.'

'She did?' It finally dawned on Megan what he was

driving at – his attempts to get Mandy Jennings to notice him.

'We've got a date,' Terry said proudly.

'Well, well,' said Megan, utterly unable to picture the two of them together. 'Good for you. Where are you taking her?'

'Well, I'm not actually going out with her, but I'm meeting her in the canteen for a coffee at eleven.'

Megan tried hard to think of something positive to say. 'So you reckon romance may be blooming then, eh?'

Again he nodded. 'She told me I was the funniest person she'd ever met.'

Terry went off, whistling as he walked down the corridor. Megan grinned, wondering if Mandy had actually understood the porcupine and chimpanzee joke. Somehow she doubted it. And she had a feeling that when Mandy had called Terry *funny* she didn't mean *funny ha-ha* but *funny peculiar*.

Ewart stifled a yawn and stared at the photograph of Ros and Sarah on his desk. It had been taken several years ago, when Sarah was still a fresh-faced young girl and Ros had been entirely happy with the life they had been living. It was hard to remember what it had been like, given the strains and tensions of recent months. That was the trouble with contentment – it was, by its very nature, unmemorable in its details, whereas periods of crisis and strife were all too difficult to forget.

Still, he was glad that Ros had gone away for a while, even though he did not relish going home to an empty house. The holiday would doubtless do her good and allow passions to cool on both sides. And by the time she returned, he would be properly settled in his new routine with the night-shift. Things would get better then, he was sure.

Ewart sighed, aware that he was trying to rationalize his own grave doubts about the future of their marriage. The truth was that a great gulf was opening up between them – a gulf largely precipitated by his inability to finally abandon medicine and retire. Ros couldn't understand that it hadn't been an entirely selfish decision – she couldn't understand that he really felt that the NHS was under grave threat and wanted to do his part in trying to help stem the tide of savage cuts which were reducing it to a parody of what it had once been. She couldn't understand his passion for the cause.

The clock on the wall showed seven-fifteen: it was time to be going home. There was a knock on the door.

'Come in,' Ewart said.

Baz Samuels and Charlie Fairhead entered. Ewart had watched Baz when she had been at work on the cardiac arrest, and he had been thoroughly impressed by her efforts, even though the man had died.

'Well,' said Charlie, 'the day shift Sister's been briefed on the cross-over patients, so we're not needed till tonight. We're just off. You coming too?'

Ewart nodded. 'Everyone else gone home?'

'Yes,' Charlie replied. 'I just saw Megan leaving. She was grinning all over her face. I reckon that woman friend of hers upstairs must be pulling through.'

'Well,' said Ewart, 'that's good news anyway.'

'You sound a bit down,' Baz observed.

'Just tired.'

'Charlie and I are going to have breakfast in a café just down the road. Care to join us?'

He thought about it, then said, 'Why not?'

'Why not?' he said, nodding.

He put his coat on and they departed, heading down the corridor. The day-shift staff had all arrived, looking crisp and businesslike in their fresh uniforms. Ewart felt crumpled and jaded, as if he had spent the night dossing on a park bench. But at the same time there was a sense of elation: they had coped, and coped well, with a very busy first night, and the sense of calm and order which now prevailed was a testament to their efforts.

Outside it was a brisk morning, the first hint of autumn in the air. Stan and Susie were outside.

'Good morning!' Stan said to them, smiling brightly. 'It is how we say "Good night" on this shift, yes?'

'I suppose so,' Ewart said.

'This is a good new team, Mr Plimmer, and I think we will have much comfort and joy together, no? And you, Doctor Baz – will I see you here again?'

'I don't think so,' Baz said.

'That is a great shame. You fit here like the glove.'

'You see?' Charlie said to her. 'How can you let us down?'

'Hey,' Baz said. 'You're all ganging up on me.'

'Then change your mind.'

'One night in a madhouse is enough for me.'

She said this jokingly rather than dismissively, but Ewart pretended to take the comment seriously: 'Don't you think the work we do here is important?'

'Of course I do. It's very important.'

'Then why not be part of it – on a permanent basis?'

'It's nothing personal – I just have other things I want to do with my career.'

'No one's asking for a permanent commitment,' he told her. 'Just a few weeks or months would do. Until we can sort out a proper replacement.'

'This is blackmail,' she protested, 'and I refuse to discuss it further on an empty stomach.'

'We're going for breakfast,' Charlie said to Stan and Susie. 'Want to come along as well?'

Stan shook his head. 'Thank you, but no. I am walking Susie to her bus-stop.'

'I think he fancies me,' Susie said lightly. 'He's a bit of a Casanova.'

'I am simply a romantic,' Stan protested. 'Beauty is everywhere, and to see it is to adore it.'

'Who are you quoting this time?' Susie asked him.

'The greatest genius of them all – Stanislaw Dabrowska.'

He and Susie departed. Just then an ambulance drove across the forecourt. Mute was at the wheel, and beside her was Ponting. He wound down the window and called to Charlie: 'How's that pair of clowns who gave everyone food-poisoning?'

'Still suffering,' Charlie called back.

'Hah,' said Ponting with a malevolent grin, 'serves them right.'

'You still all right, then?'

'Didn't eat any sausages, did I?'

'We've just had another one in who didn't either,' Charlie told him. 'He'd been eating egg sandwiches.'

A look of horror suddenly filled Ponting's face. Ewart caught a secret grin on Mute's lips as she drove the ambulance away.

'You made that up,' Baz said to Charlie.

'Course I did,' he told her. 'Ponting's been moaning and complaining about the business all night – getting very pompous and insufferable about the whole affair. Mute hasn't had a moment's peace all evening, so I decided to shut him up for half an hour or so. Let him stew in his own digestive juices, so to speak.'

'Mute looked as if she was wise to it,' Ewart remarked.

'She's smarter than Ponting,' Charlie said. 'People who listen rather than talk often are.'

They were walking across the forecourt. Suddenly Charlie halted, staring towards his car. A blonde woman in her late twenties was standing in front of it, looking straight at him. There was a faint, rather tentative, smile on her lips.

'Uh,' Charlie said to Ewart and Baz, 'I think I'm going to have to pass up on that breakfast. Do you mind?'

Ewart had never met Charlie's girlfriend, but he guessed that this was her.

'That's all right,' he said. 'I'll make sure Baz is well looked after.'

Charlie turned to Baz. 'See you on the shift in twelve hours' time, then.'

'I wouldn't bet on it,' Baz replied.

'I'm counting on you,' he said to Ewart, 'to smooth-talk her into it.'

'I'll do my best,' Ewart promised with a smile.

They walked off, leaving him to approach the woman.

'Girlfriend?' Baz said.

'Looks like it,' Ewart replied. 'I've got a feeling that they've had a tiff and that it's now reconciliation time. Easier to bounce back when you're young, isn't it?'

'That sounds like a cry from the heart, Ewart.'

They had reached the car, and he fitted his key into the door.

'Stay with us long enough,' he said, 'and I'll tell you the story of my life.'

* * *

Charlie walked slowly across to Liz.

'You're up early,' he said.

'I couldn't sleep,' she told him. 'I wanted to see you.'

'Get a bus, did you?'

'I walked.'

Charlie lit a cigarette and watched Ewart's car pull away.

'How did it go?' Liz asked.

'It went.'

'Listen,' she said. 'I'm sorry.'

'Yeah. I am, too.'

'I don't want us to break up.'

Charlie was not looking at her. He took his car keys from his pocket, jingled them in his hand. Said nothing.

'Charlie,' she said. 'It was a mistake.'

'What was? Doing it, or telling me about it?'

She sighed. 'Give me a cigarette.'

'Buy your own.' But he got the packet out anyway and offered her one. He was forced to face her as he did so, and she made sure she caught his eye.

'I love you, you know,' she said.

'You've got a funny way of showing it.'

'I never claimed to be perfect. Can you say you've been one hundred per cent faithful to me since we've been together?'

'As it happens, I can.'

'And you've never been tempted by anyone else?'

'Of course I have. But that's the point. Temptation's one thing. Actually doing it's another.'

'You know, Charlie – deep down you're a puritan.'

He turned on her angrily. 'Don't try and give me any of that psychological crap, Liz! Don't try and make me feel guilty!'

'I'm sorry.'

224

Suddenly he knew what was really bothering him. The truth was, he didn't actually believe that she'd gone to bed with Brownlow.

'You made it up, didn't you?'

'What?' she asked.

'You didn't sleep with Brownlow at all. It was just some kind of test, to see how I'd react.'

She looked genuinely surprised. 'Would you rather believe that?'

'It's not a question of trying to fool myself – I believe what I see and hear. When I walked in on you and Brownlow in *The Green Pagoda*, he had all the answers, and he didn't strike me as someone who was making it up as he went along. He wasn't guilty or evasive – he was bloody angry, just like someone who was really innocent would be. He hadn't slept with you.'

Liz was silent. But the logic of Charlie's argument now led him to an even more unwelcome supposition.

'Maybe *you* propositioned him, and he said no. Maybe that's why you felt guilty about it.'

'No, Charlie.'

'Did you really want the job that much?'

It was her turn to get angry. 'It was nothing to do with the job, Charlie! And whether you like it or not, it happened!'

'So you're proud of it, are you?'

'No! Would I be here if I was?'

A couple of nurses were walking past, and they turned their heads at the sounds of the raised voices. Charlie took a deep drag of his cigarette, dropped the butt on the floor, crushed it under the heel of his shoe.

'Charlie,' Liz said, 'let's go home.'

'Why? So that we can continue the argument there?'

'I want us to forget it. Accept what's happened, yes, but put it in the past.'

'That's easy for you to say.'

'We could always get married.'

He looked at her. 'You've got to be joking. That would give you a new option, wouldn't it? Adultery rather than fornication.'

He had wanted to wound her, but he immediately knew that he had gone too far. Without a word she tossed aside the cigarette he had given her and walked off.

As he stood there, staring after her, Charlie was gripped with the certainty that she was now walking out of his life. But they had been together for so long, had shared so many good times, that the idea seemed unreal. He watched her until she had disappeared around the corner of a building. She had not looked back.

Charlie got into his car and started up the engine. He drove slowly out of the hospital forecourt, turning left on to the main road.

Liz was walking along the pavement, about a hundred yards away. Charlie stayed in second gear and finally pulled up just ahead of her.

As she came abreast of the car, he reached across and opened the passenger door. She had halted, was waiting for him to speak.

'Get in,' he said.

Children in uniform were on their way to school as Ewart turned his car into his street; their day was beginning just as his was ending. Working the night-shift often made you feel as if you were living your life in reverse.

He parked outside his gate and got out of the car. The first thing he noticed was that Joyce's garden had been repaired. The gouges on the lawn could scarcely be seen, and the rose bushes had been planted in place of the flowers which had been torn up.

A net curtain had fluttered at one of Joyce's windows, and now she emerged, smartly dressed in a dark blue skirt with a matching jacket over a cream silk blouse. She was carrying a bottle of milk.

'This is for you,' she said, walking briskly up to him. 'To replace the one I borrowed.'

Ewart didn't need it, but it would have been ungracious to refuse.

'Thank you,' he said, accepting the bottle.

'Have you just come off duty?' she asked.

'More or less. I'm looking forward to a few hours' sleep now. How are you feeling?'

'I'm coping. That's what we do, isn't it? Cope.'

Ewart gave a smile which he hoped looked sympathetic.

'I'm going away,' she said. 'After I've seen Dr Mowbray this morning. I'm going to visit Donald's mother in St Ives for a few weeks.'

'That sounds nice.'

'It will be. She doesn't like him any more than I do. We spend the whole time bitching about him.'

Now Ewart's smile was unforced. 'Everyone's taking holidays,' he said. 'Looks like I missed the boat.'

'You don't mind, though, do you? I can tell. You love your work.'

'"Love" may be putting it a bit strongly.'

'Well, you have a vocation, anyway. It means a lot to you.'

'I suppose it does.'

'And a good family life. I envy you, I really do.'

As if embarrassed by what she had said, she turned

227

and moved quickly off, calling to him that she'd see him when she got back from St Ives. How little we know about one another, Ewart thought. Then he headed up the pathway to the door of his empty house.

18

Charlie had overslept, and he was late getting to the Church Field for the soccer match. By the time he arrived, there were only fifteen minutes left of the game.

A sizeable crowd had gathered around the edges of field – perhaps a hundred people – and Charlie positioned himself next to a knot of youngsters who were all wearing the amber and black scarves of the St Andrews Strollers. Eastmead, the team they were playing, were in blue and white.

A steady drizzle had been falling most of the afternoon, but support for both sides was substantial not only numerically but vocally. The kids were yelling and screaming for their respective sides while passing around packets of crisps and big bottles of lemonade and Tizer. Charlie glanced around at the adults present, but he didn't see anyone he recognized apart from Clive, who was standing alone near the touchline, shouting orders to his troops. There was no point in disturbing him until the game was over.

'What's the score?' he asked a boy standing next to him.

'One-all,' came the reply.

'How long left?'

The boy glanced at a Darth Vader watch on his wrist. 'Ten minutes. Come on, the Strollers!'

Charlie recognized Errol, who was leading the Strollers' attack, and Bobby, who was playing at the heart of the defence. Both boys were well smeared with mud, evidence of their commitment to the game. The pitch itself was turning slowly into a morass, and the rain was coming down more heavily.

Charlie contemplated making a dash for the old pavilion, but he decided against it with so little time left in the match. Eastmead mounted an attack, the ball being crossed from the wing towards the tall striker who headed it sharply down towards the goal.

The Strollers' goalkeeper was beaten, but Bobby stuck out a foot to clear the ball from the line. Charlie could see a big grin on Clive's face when the danger vanished as a result of his son's clearance. A minute or so later, Errol was brought down in Eastmead's penalty area, and now Clive was staring with alarm as his other son lay crumpled in the mud.

But Errol sprang up quickly even as the referee blew his whistle and pointed to the penalty spot.

The Strollers' captain stepped up to take the kick. Half of their supporters in the crowd were urging him to place the kick, the other half to blast it as hard as he could at the goal. But the boy ignored them, running forward and kicking the ball both hard and accurately past the diving Eastmead goalkeeper. 2-1.

In the few minutes that remained, the Strollers were forced to defend furiously, and Clive grew increasingly agitated, stalking up and down the touchline and yelling at his team to stay vigilant. Charlie was surprised at the seriousness and fervour which he was displaying; the team obviously was for Clive as much a passion as a hobby. Charlie glanced at his watch: they were playing injury time.

One of the Strollers now booted the ball right out of the field and over the low stone wall of the church graveyard. The teams had to pause while it was being retrieved, adding to the tension. Clive was pacing up and down the touchline, and then he walked over to a tall woman whom Charlie recognized as his wife, Leah. Charlie was now in earshot of them, and he heard Leah say, 'Calm down, will you? It won't be the end of the world if they lose.'

'Lose?' said Clive, as if this was unthinkable. 'I'm worried enough about Eastmead equalizing. If they manage to score two goals, I'll shoot myself!'

Charlie grinned, huddling into his windcheater as the rain came down still more heavily. Despite the weather, he was glad of the game, glad of the chance to be distracted from the continuing uncertainties of his relationship with Liz.

Nothing had really been resolved between them, even though they had driven home together from the hospital and immediately gone to bed. They had made love with as much passion as ever, and yet a part of him had remained detached throughout it all, as though he couldn't let go fully any more. Even though he was still uncertain that anything had actually happened, the truth was that the Gavin Brownlow affair had made him lose a crucial element of trust in Liz. He wasn't sure whether he would be able to recover that. But it wouldn't be for want of trying.

The ball had been recovered, and now play resumed. Eastmead launched a final frantic attack, and again the ball was scrambled away from the goal-line. Then suddenly the referee was blowing his whistle and waving an arm in the air.

It was over. The Strollers had won the Cup.

Clive already had a big grin on his face, and he was being congratulated by Leah. He glanced in Charlie's direction, and Charlie shouted a 'Well done!' before the rest of the crowd converged around him and his players.

Suddenly Charlie heard a familiar voice shout, 'It's drier in here.'

He turned. Standing in the old pavilion was Duffy, and with her was Ewart. And Megan. And Baz Samuels.

Charlie hurried up the rickety wooden steps. Everyone was in a huddle around one of the windows, avoiding the rain that was dripping in through various holes in the roof.

'Didn't think you were going to make it,' Duffy said.

'Forgot to set the alarm.' Charlie looked at the others. 'Well, this is cosy. The gang's all here.'

His gaze settled on Baz. She was wearing a fawn raincoat, its big collar turned up around her head.

'Nice to see you again,' he said.

'You'll be seeing a lot more of her from now on,' remarked Megan. 'Ewart's persuaded her to join the shift on a permanent basis.'

'Only for a few months,' Baz was quick to say. 'Until you can find a permanent replacement.'

'You old charmer,' Charlie said to Ewart. 'How did you manage that?'

Ewart was smiling beatifically, and only now did Charlie notice that he was wearing a slender pair of earphones, a wire trailing down to the inside pocket of his jacket.

'He's wired for sound,' Duffy said. 'Bought himself a Sony Walkman to cheer himself up, he said.'

Ewart had obviously not heard Charlie, but now he removed the earphones after twiddling with something inside his jacket.

'Excellent,' he remarked. 'The sound quality is excellent. I shall have to transfer all my records on to tape. What were you saying, Charlie?'

'I was wondering how you finally persuaded Baz to stay with us.'

But it was Baz herself who said: 'He just reminded me of how much the unit is needed and what the threats of closures can mean to the hospital service. If I can help the unit justify its existence, then it's worthwhile. It's no good complaining about cuts if you're not prepared to do anything about it.'

'You see?' said Ewart, 'I didn't really have to persuade her at all. Just give her the facts, which speak for themselves.'

At the edge of the football field the presentation was now being arranged, several well-dressed men and women standing under big rainbow-coloured golfing umbrellas. At their head was a florid-faced man in his fifties. He was holding a small golden cup, and they were close enough to hear him address Clive and his mud-splattered team.

'I had great pleasure in sponsoring this cup,' he began, 'on behalf of Samuels Investments. It is always gratifying to be able to put our names to worthwhile social events, especially when they involve youth.'

'Yeck,' murmured Duffy. 'What a pompous oaf.'

'He's my father,' Baz said.

Duffy blushed deeply, looking shame-faced.

'Don't worry,' Baz told her, 'I agree with you – he's a windbag who'll use any excuse to publicize himself. He'd love to see me settled down in some expensive private practice and he's always trying to get me to meet The Right People, whoever they're supposed to be. He actually asked me to come along today to present the cup. Can you believe it?'

Charlie looked at her. 'Does he know you're here?'

'No fear. And I'm keeping out of sight. That's my mother next to him – the one picking lumps of mud off the heels of her shoes.'

After a lengthy preamble, Baz's father finally presented the cup to Clive and his team amid much cheering.

'We ought to go and congratulate Clive,' Ewart said. 'You coming, Baz?'

She shook her head. 'I'm going home to snatch a couple of hours' sleep before we're on duty again.'

'Did I detect a trace of anticipation in your voice at the thought of it?' asked Charlie.

'God, I think there was. Maybe I ought to come in tonight not as staff but as a patient – a suitable case for treatment.'

'Barbara?' said a voice from outside. 'Is that you in there?'

Baz had immediately ducked back out of sight, but her father was peering towards the pavilion window. He started forward, dragging his wife with him. She was dressed in a lilac outfit with matching shoes, and she was vainly striving to keep one of the golfing umbrellas aloft as she was whisked forward.

Baz's father was clearly determined to corner his daughter inside the pavilion, but he had not accounted for the muddiness of the terrain and his wife's stiletto heels. In his haste he waded straight into a particularly swampy patch of grass. Baz's mother's heels sank deep into the sod, upending both of them so that they sprawled face-down in a muddy pool.

From the pavilion came sounds of stifled laughter. Charlie looked around for Baz but she was already gone, hurrying across the football field towards the church.

234

'You won't find sanctuary there!' he called after her as she disappeared behind its redbrick facade.

But seconds later a white Peugot 205 GTI pulled out from behind the building. Baz was at the wheel, and she gave him a cheery wave as she drove off at speed.

<u>CASUALTY</u>

The Early Years

Laura Waring

Megan Roach is the backbone of Holby's Casualty
department. Her down-to-earth Irish nature and
boundless energy make her a favourite with staff and
patients alike, and her husband and teenage sons would
be lost without her love and devotion.

But after years of caring for others, Megan must at last
face up to the fact that she is in need of care herself.
When a serious illness is diagnosed she must confront it –
though in her usual way she tries to avoid fuss and
attention. But for all those who love her, this is their
chance to prove that she is irreplaceable.

From the nation's best loved hospital series, the
immensely popular characters of CASUALTY here live
out the dramas that the cameras don't see.

CASUALTY

Swings and Roundabouts

Lynda Del Sasso

Charlie Fairhead is the joker of Holby Casualty. Always
there to relieve the strain of a heavy shift with his wry
humour, he is nevertheless fiercely committed to his work.
Often the bearer of bad news, he never shirks his
responsibilities and is always ready with a shoulder to cry
on for colleagues and public alike.

But behind his happy-go-lucky exterior, Charlie's private
life is empty, and he longs to have someone to share the
good times. So when he and a friend chance on romance,
it could be that his hopes are at last coming true. But
before he can enjoy love, Charlie must consult his
conscience, and a hard choice lies before him . . .

From the nation's best loved hospital series, the
immensely popular characters of CASUALTY here live
out the dramas that the cameras don't see.

Warner now offers an exciting range of quality titles by both established and new authors. All of the books in this series are available from:
Little, Brown and Company (UK) Limited,
P.O. Box 11,
Falmouth,
Cornwall TR10 9EN.

Alternatively you may fax your order to the above address. Fax No. 0326 376423.

Payments can be made as follows: Cheque, postal order (payable to Little, Brown and Company) or by credit cards, Visa/Access. Do not send cash or currency. UK customers: and B.F.P.O.: please send a cheque or postal order (no currency) and allow £1.00 for postage and packing for the first book, plus 50p for the second book, plus 30p for each additional book up to a maximum charge of £3.00 (7 books plus).

Overseas customers including Ireland, please allow £2.00 for postage and packing for the first book, plus £1.00 for the second book, plus 50p for each additional book.

NAME (Block Letters) ....

ADDRESS..

....

☐ I enclose my remittance for _____

☐ I wish to pay by Access/Visa Card

Number ⬜⬜⬜⬜⬜⬜⬜⬜⬜⬜⬜⬜⬜⬜⬜⬜⬜⬜⬜

Card Expiry Date ⬜⬜⬜⬜